NO MORE
SWEET
SURRENDER

NO MORE SWEET SURRENDER

BY

CAITLIN CREWS

First published in Great Britain 2013
by Mills & Boon, an imprint of Harlequin (UK) Limited.
Large Print edition 2013
Harlequin (UK) Limited, Eton House,
18-24 Paradise Road, Richmond, Surrey TW9 1SR

© Caitlin Crews 2013

ISBN: 978 0 263 23196 0

Printed and bound in Great Britain
by CPI Antony Rowe, Chippenham, Wiltshire

This book could not have been written without the wonderful ladies on Sharon Kendrick's gorgeous writing course at the Watermill in Posara, Italy. Thank you so much for all of your encouragement and enthusiasm—it made all the difference!

Victoria Parker, Jennifer Drogell, Lorna Sweeney, Louise Okafor, Ann Burnell, Shirley Knight and Jane Carling—this one is for you.

Special thanks to the incomparable Sharon Kendrick and the always inspiring Jane Porter: I'll always treasure what amounted to a Master Class in writing with the two of you—in glorious Tuscany, no less!

And to my private and personal ninja Jeff Johnson, for teaching me about martial arts—and how to breathe.

CHAPTER ONE

ONE moment Professor Miranda Sweet was trying to slip through the scrum of people outside the Georgetown University Conference Center, where she'd just delivered her keynote speech to attendees of the Global Summit to End Violence in Media, and the next, someone was gripping her arms. Hard. Mean. Enough to bruise.

She clenched her hands tight on the handle of her bag as she was swung around, wholly against her will—and then there was a man's face much too close to hers, invading her space. The warm spring afternoon in Washington, D.C., seemed cold and hostile, suddenly. She had the hectic impression of angry words with a belligerent scowl, and the swift and terrifying understanding that this man wished her ill.

And like that, she was a girl again. Helpless and scared and cowering in the corner while her father raged and smashed things, then turned his furious glare on her. Just like the girl she'd been then, she shook.

"What—" she began, shocked to hear the quaver in her voice that reminded her of that helpless version of herself she'd thought she'd buried almost ten years ago.

"You need to listen instead of talk, for once," the strange man growled at her, his words heavily accented.

Miranda's instinct was to apologize, to obey. To cower and agree—anything to deflect his anger, to appease it—

But then there was another hand, this one smooth and gentle against the small of her back, though it was also undeniably strong. It felt almost possessive as it drew her inexorably away from the man who'd grabbed her and brought her up against a broad male chest. Miranda lost her breath. She knew she should have protested—screamed, swung out with her bag, perhaps—but something stopped her. It was the strangest sensation, as if she was safe, despite all evidence to the contrary. The hard fingers around the tender flesh of her upper arms dropped away, at last, and she tilted her head back to blink in astonishment at the man who still held her close to him.

Like some kind of protector. Like a lover. But she knew who he was, she realized in astonishment. And she knew he was neither of those things.

"You have made a mistake," he told the other man, his Russian-flavored voice cold.

He recognized her, too, Miranda knew when he looked down at her again. She saw the flare of it in his deep black eyes, and despite herself, she felt an echoing chill of that recognition shiver down her spine and shake its way through her. She had studied this man, taught his films and his fights in her classes. She had discussed what she felt he represented, at length, in print and on television. But she had never met him before. She had certainly never *touched* him.

He was Ivan Korovin. *The* Ivan Korovin. Former undefeated mixed martial arts champion, current Hollywood action movie darling, famous for being exactly what he was and everything Miranda hated: unapologetically aggressive, casually brutal and celebrated hither and yon for both.

He was the tall, dark and entirely too handsome walking embodiment of everything she'd built her career fighting against.

The angry man barked out something then that

she didn't need to speak Russian to understand was cruel and vicious. She'd heard that tone before, and she felt it like a blow to her stomach just the same.

Miranda felt every famous inch of Ivan Korovin, pressed against her as he was—hot and hard and not, it turned out, air-brushed in any way beneath the luxurious suit he wore—stiffen with tension.

"Be very careful you do not insult what belongs to me," he warned in that low voice of his that was richer and more stirring in person than on film. It seemed to wash over her like a heat rash, making her skin prickle in reaction. It confused her. It came far too close to scaring her in a wholly different way.

It made her almost miss the impossible, absurd thing he'd just said.

What belongs to him?

"I do not mean to trespass, of course," the other man said then, his small, mean eyes still fastened on Miranda in a way that made her shift uneasily in what no doubt looked like Ivan's embrace. Though she did nothing to extricate herself, and on some level she thought less of herself for her own cowardice. "It does me no good to have you as my enemy."

Ivan's smile then was like one of the weapons they claimed he didn't even need, so lethal was he without them. With only his hands and his skill. "Then be certain you never lay hands on her again, Guberev."

Miranda could *feel* it when he spoke, this man made of brute force and extreme physical prowess, the dark timbre of it rumbling through her like an expensive engine, powerful and low, making parts of her she'd never paid much attention to before seem to…*spark.*

What was the matter with her? She much preferred brains to brawn, thank you. She always had, due to her father's reliance on his superior strength and size throughout her violent childhood under his deceptively well-manicured roof in tony Greenwich, Connecticut. And besides… this was *Ivan Korovin*!

Miranda had been a regular face on the news and talk-show circuit ever since she'd published her doctoral dissertation as a surprisingly well-received book two years back. *Caveman Worship* focused on the widespread hero worship of particularly brutal professional sports figures. She considered herself a much-needed voice of reason in a tragically violent world that adored brutes like the famously reclusive and tight-lipped Ivan Korovin—both the one he'd been in his mixed martial arts days and the one he'd played in the incredibly violent Jonas Dark action films for the past few years since his retirement from the ring.

She pushed back against his absurdly chiseled chest, ignoring the way all of that smooth muscle felt against her palms. She hardly heard the other man's insincere apologies then, because she was caught up in Ivan Korovin's searing midnight gaze instead. And suddenly, a wild staccato sort of pounding seemed to beat through her veins, thick and sweet and dizzying, and she thought her legs might give out from underneath her.

It turned out that the camera did him no favors. On screen he looked tough, dangerous. A lethal killing machine, forged in a bloodthirsty fire. He was usually half-naked and extravagantly tattooed—an extraordinarily powerful *punch* of sheer masculinity who could mow through his opponents like they were made of butter, and usually did.

A Neanderthal, Miranda had always thought.

And had felt comfortable calling him in a variety of public places.

And he was certainly that, as well as tall and hard-packed with all of that sleek and solid muscle, as expected—but this close Miranda could see that he was surprisingly, shockingly beautiful in his ruthlessly male way, for all that he was also so clearly battered from all of his years of fighting. The nose he'd obviously broken a few times couldn't take away from the perfect lushness of his mouth. The scar on his forehead faded next to the sheer glory of his cheekbones. The gorgeous, expertly tailored suit he wore made him a kind of elegant suggestion of a threat instead of the direct one she'd always considered him, and she was completely thrown by the surprising gleam of intelligence in his too-dark eyes.

It was like falling over a cliff into a very deep, very dark abyss. Miranda forgot about the angry man who'd started this by grabbing her. She forgot the old, awful memories he'd stirred up, and her own ingrained cowardice. She forgot everything. Even herself, as if there was nothing in all the world but the way Ivan Korovin was looking at her.

And Miranda never forgot herself. She never

lost control. *Never.* She was appalled that she had to remind herself of that.

"What *belongs* to you?" she asked, echoing back his words, trying to regain her balance. "Did you just refer to me as if I'm some kind of *possession*? Like a goat?"

There was no reason he should have smiled like that, that dark quirk of his dangerously beautiful mouth. There was even less reason that she should have felt it like a touch against her skin, long and lingering. And she certainly shouldn't have felt an answering sort of echo, a deep and irresistible pull, low in her belly.

It occurred to her then that he was far more dangerous than even she'd believed, and she'd only last week called him *the bogeyman* on national television.

"I am a very possessive man," he told her, his accent making the words seem almost like a caress. He flicked a hard look at the other man who still stood there, reeking of malice and terrible cologne, then returned his dark, brooding gaze to Miranda's. And she felt it. Everywhere. "It is a terrible flaw."

He tugged her closer to him with embarrassing ease then, plastering her against him as if she had no will of her own, which was, frighteningly, exactly how she felt—and then he simply bent his head and claimed her mouth with his.

She had no time to think.

His lush and beautiful mouth was shockingly carnal against hers, wicked and clever, demanding and hot.

Physical.

He took her over, as if it was his right. As if she'd begged him to do it. She felt his hard hand against the side of her face, guiding her mouth to his with an easy, almost offhanded mastery that made her whole body pull tight in sensual delight. Heat exploded inside of her, volcanic and stunning. She didn't fight. She didn't so much as whimper. *She didn't even want to.* She simply... let this man she imagined disliked her as much as she did him kiss her as if they were moments away from tumbling into the nearest bed. She simply surrendered to his endless, impossible, unspeakably erotic kiss—

When he finally lifted his head, his black eyes were burning with the same fire Miranda felt consuming her. There was a ringing in her ears, and she couldn't feel her own hands where they were braced against his great wall of a chest. She had the vague thought that she might actually be having a heart attack. And then, a moment later, she knew she only wished she was—the better to avoid, forever, what had just happened.

What he'd done and, worse, what she'd felt. What she hadn't so much as offered up a token protest against. What was still raging through her like an electrical storm, knocking down power lines and leaving her stunned.

He muttered a pretty word that she was certain was a curse, but speared through her like a wild flame. *"Milaya."*

It was something about the way he said it, or perhaps it was that stirring, considering look in his black gaze. It flipped some kind of switch in her, and what washed over her then was nothing as simple as *fire*. It was dark and complicated and new, and left her feeling starkly, nakedly vulnerable, and worse, convinced that he could *see it*—

For a wild, panicked moment then, she thought she really had burst into flames after all. Bright lights exploded all around her and she realized, dazedly, that they'd been flashing for some time.

It took her one ragged breath, then another, to understand that it was not his kiss—though she could still feel it storming through her, shuddering and spinning out that wild heat, making her something like nauseated and restless and humiliatingly desperate for more, all at once—or even that demanding, challenging way he was looking at her now. It wasn't his hard, capable hands that still held her against him. It wasn't even that sudden slap of fearful vulnerability that she was still too afraid he could read.

It was the cameras. The paparazzi who hung on Ivan Korovin's every taciturn word and calculated deed, recording the entire insane situation for posterity and plastering it all over those glossy supermarket magazines. And they'd certainly gotten a show today, hadn't they?

The angry man was gone, as if he'd never been. There was only Ivan Korovin and the aftereffects of that searing kiss. And Miranda was forced to face the unsavory truth: she'd just been caught with one of her staunchest opponents, the man who had once dismissed her by calling her *a tiny, yipping dog* on a famous nightly talk show to the sound of much approving applause.

Kissing him, no less. In public.

At an international summit teeming with policy makers, academics and delegates from at least fifteen countries, all as deeply and philosophically opposed to everything he stood for as she was.

Miranda had to assume that every last moment of it was on film. The avid, delighted expressions of the jostling throng of reporters surrounding her assured her that it was.

Which meant, she knew with a terrible sinking sensation inside, that her entire career had just taken one of the knockout body blows for which Ivan Korovin was so famous.

To say nothing of the rest of her.

If looks could kill, Ivan reflected a short time later, the redheaded professor would have eviscerated him while the cameras still rolled.

He'd moved fast after he'd kissed her, that serious lapse in judgment he was still having difficulty justifying to himself. He'd had his security people clear a path into the conference hotel. Once inside, he'd directed her into a secluded seating area behind a riot of plants.

She hadn't looked at him again and he'd imagined she was fighting with a truth that must have been wholly unpalatable for this self-appointed harpy who fought against all he wanted to accomplish: she owed him her thanks. Her gratitude. A better man might not have taken such satisfaction in that, but then, Ivan had never pretended to be anything but what he was. What would be the point?

But when she lifted her gaze to his—that slap of dark jade that he found intrigued him far more than it should, far more than he was comfortable admitting, even to himself—he understood that she had no intention of thanking him.

She was furious. At him.

He wasn't surprised. But he was too much the fighter, still and always, not to see a flare of temper in another and want to meet it. Dominate it and control it.

Her.

After all, he thought with a certain grimness, he owed her. She'd been making his life difficult for going on two years now. Was there any name she hadn't called him? Any lie she wasn't prepared to tell to make her point, no matter what it cost him? Her voice echoed in his ears even now, painting him in the worst possible light, turning public opinion against him, announcing to anyone who would listen that he was exactly the kind of monster he'd spent his life fighting—

Oh, yes. He owed her.

"What," she asked, her voice dripping with a mix of ice and fury, as if he was nothing more than a naughty student misbehaving in one of her classes, as if she was unaware of her own peril, "was *that*?"

"Did I startle you?" he asked idly, as if fighting off deep boredom. As if he'd already half forgotten her. It made her dark eyes glint green with outrage. "I thought it best to act swiftly."

She moved up from her seat and on to her feet. She was not one of those drearily serious American women who feared heels, apparently. Hers were sleek and sharp and at least three inches high, and she looked entirely too comfortable in them as she stood there with a certain bravado meant, he knew, to tell him without words that she refused to be dominated by him.

But it was too late. He knew she tasted like fire.

"You grabbed me," she bit out with that same controlled flash of temper that made him think of long, icy winters. And how they melted into summer, all the same. "You manhandled me. You…"

Her face flushed then, and Ivan found himself unaccountably fascinated by the stain of red that worked its way from her smooth cheeks down to her elegant neck. Kisses could lie, he knew. But not that telltale flush of color, making her eyes glitter and her breath come quicker. He couldn't look away.

"Kissed you," he affirmed.

He should not find an opponent *fascinating.* Especially not *this* opponent, who had judged him so harshly and unfairly condemned him years ago. This particular opponent whose well-timed, perfectly placed barbs always seemed to hit at exactly the right moment to make him seem like some kind of deranged comic book character— hardly the reputation he wanted to have when he needed to use his celebrity brand to bolster his brand-new charity foundation. He certainly should not make the fatal mistake of noticing she was a woman, and far more compelling than simply a voice of dissent.

"That is true," he said darkly. "I did all of those things."

"How dare you?"

"I dare many things." He shrugged. "As I believe you have noted in nauseating detail in your cable television interviews."

She glared at him, and Ivan took the opportunity to study this nemesis of his from up close. She was made up of those delicate bones and graceful, patrician lines that made his blood sing, entirely against his will. She was tall for a woman, and slim, though nothing like the kind of skinny he had been too poor for too long to associate with anything but desperation. But he could see, now, that she was neither as fragile nor as brittle as he'd assumed. Her hair was a long, sleek fall of a very dark red, captivating and unusual next to those mysterious eyes. The dark trouser suit she wore was both professional and decidedly, deliciously feminine, and he found himself reliving the brief, sweet crush of her small yet perfectly rounded breasts against his chest when he'd kissed her.

It was the closest he'd come to pure *want* in longer than he could remember.

He told himself he hated it.

"Dmitry Guberev is a remarkably unpleasant man who thinks his new money makes him strong," Ivan said curtly, deeply annoyed with himself. "He had a very short, very pathetic career as a fighter in Kiev, and is now some kind of fight promoter. I convinced him to leave you alone in the only way he was likely to understand. If you choose to take offense at that, I can't stop you."

"By telling him I'm *yours*?" The icy emphasis she put on the last word poked at him, made him want to heat her up—and he knew how, now, didn't he? He knew exactly how to kiss her, how to taste her, how to angle his mouth over hers for a wilder, better fit. "How medieval. Your *what*, may I ask?"

"I believe he thinks you are my lover," Ivan said silkily, testing out the word on his tongue even as he tested the idea in his head, and despite the fact he knew it was as insane as it was impossible. Self-sabotage at its finest. This woman was poison. But he couldn't seem to stop goading her, even so. "Not my goat."

"I didn't ask you to charge in on your white horse and save me," she said, her fascinating gaze a shade or two darker, which Ivan took to be the remnants of that same fire he couldn't seem to put out of his head. Her cultured American voice remained smooth.

She sounded like those dark gray pearls she wore in an elegant loop around her neck, smooth and supple and expensive, impossibly aristocratic. She was well out of the reach of a desperately poor kid who'd grown up hard in Nizhny Novgorod when it was still known as Gorky, the

Russian word for *bitter*—which was precisely how he recalled those dark, cold years. Maybe that was why she got beneath his skin; it had been a long time now since anyone had dismissed him the way this woman did. He didn't like it.

Or, he reminded himself pointedly, her.

"I didn't need your help," she continued, all offended dignity, as if he hadn't seen that look in her eyes in the moment before he'd involved himself. As if he hadn't seen that painfully familiar flash of something too much like helpless misery wash over her expressive face.

But she wasn't his responsibility, he told himself now. She had made herself his enemy, and he should remember that above all things.

"Perhaps not." He shrugged as if it was no matter to him, which, in fact, it shouldn't have been. "But I know Guberev. He is an ugly little man, and he would have done far worse if I had not stepped in." His brows rose in challenge. "How are your arms where he grabbed you, Professor? Do they hurt?"

She looked confused for a moment, as if she hadn't yet taken the time to catalogue her own pains. She slid her hands up over her arms, hugging herself gently, and the idea of Guberev's marks on her skin, Ivan discovered as she winced slightly, bothered him. A lot.

"I'm fine," she said. She dropped her hands back to her sides, shifted her weight from one foot to the other, and Ivan had spent too much of his life reading body language not to understand that she was far less composed than she appeared. He shouldn't have taken any kind of satisfaction in that, either. "And while I appreciate your urge to help, if that's what it was, you'll understand that I can't condone the method you used."

"It was extreme, perhaps," he allowed. It was certainly that. Why had he kissed her? Like so many bullies, Guberev was at heart a coward, as Ivan well knew, having been forced to contend with the slimy little man in the mixed martial arts world for years. What Guberev might want to do to a weaker creature like this woman, given the chance, he would not dare to do in the presence of someone stronger. That Ivan was there should have been enough. Why had he taken it further? "But effective."

"Effective for whom?" she asked, that smooth voice finally betraying her tension. "You may have single-handedly derailed my entire career. I can only assume that was your goal. What better way to undermine the things I say about you than to render me no more than one of the sexual playthings you famously run through like water?"

As if he had to fight like that, dirty and underhanded. He was Ivan Korovin. He was a champion and a movie star and neither by accident, despite her insinuations. He'd put in hours upon hours of grueling training to become the fighter he was. He'd become fluent in English and had minimized his accent within three years of leaving Russia. He did not *undermine*. He preferred the direct approach. He was famous for it, come to that.

"Did you become one of my sexual playthings?" he asked darkly. "I feel certain I would remember it."

"Let's be clear," she said, her voice under that smooth control of hers once more, which made him want to throw her off balance again, somehow. "I study you. You've spent your entire professional life strategically taking down your opponents, one after the next, without admitting the possibility of defeat."

He told himself the new color on her cheeks then was a result of the same stark and wild images that were currently torturing him, and had nothing to do with her *study* of him, as if he was an animal in a zoo. That wicked mouth of hers, slick and addictive. That damnable fire. Her long, graceful limbs wrapped around him. How could he find her so attractive when he knew she would destroy him in an instant, if she could? When she had already done her best to do so? But reason had nothing to do with the heat that rocketed through him. He wanted to sink his fingers into the dark fire of her hair and hear her scream his name as she came all around him, hot and wet and *his.*

Ivan despaired of himself.

"You are often called an unstoppable force," she said crisply, her chin rising as if she expected a fight, as if she thought that simple truth was an insult. "It doesn't take a great leap of imagination to conclude that you saw a way to cut me down, too. And jumped at the chance."

"I can find your work interesting, Dr. Sweet," he said, sick of himself as he tried to force the seductive, distracting images from his head, "even if I completely disagree with it. And I can disagree with it without concocting wild strategies to discredit you. I wanted to help you. I would have helped anyone in the same position. I'm sorry if you find that offensive."

She studied him for a moment, her fine brows lowered into a frown. He had that dislocating sense of being measured and found wanting, another unpleasant reminder of his unfortunate youth, his desperate, determined climb to fame. He had to take a breath, control his response, keep himself calm. Lucky for her that he had made an art of it.

"Life is not an action movie, Mr. Korovin," she said in her cool, professorial voice, as if she was rendering judgment from high on some podium instead of standing right there in front of him, within reach, her lips still slightly reddened from his. "You cannot sweep in, kiss a woman without her permission and expect accolades. You are far more likely to find yourself slapped with a harassment suit."

"Of course," he replied in that bored tone that made temper kick bright and hard in her dark jade gaze. A better man might not find the sight exhilarating. "Thank you for reminding me that I am currently in the most litigious country on earth. The next time I see you in the path of a truck, be it human or machine, I'll let it mow you down where you stand."

"I can't imagine our paths will ever cross again," she retorted, all elegant affront, which only made that dark current of *want* in him intensify. He'd felt her against him, meltingly pliant. Her heat. Her fire. He knew the truth, now, behind her high-class, overeducated front. Behind the cool way she'd ripped him into shreds for years now with every appearance of delight. It burned in him. "For which I am profoundly grateful. Now if you'll excuse me, I have to go perform some damage control, since the whole world saw me let some macho Hollywood hulk kiss me in—"

"Be honest, Professor," he interrupted her. "If you dare."

His gaze met hers. Held. And he wasn't amused or fascinated or anything that distant, suddenly. It was as if she'd woken that part of him he'd thought long buried with her cool disdain and her quiet horror at his touch—like he'd polluted her somehow. Like he was one of the very monsters he fought against. As if everything that hung in the balance here didn't matter anymore, save the very real response he'd tasted on her lips.

He knew fire when it burned him. God help them both.

"You kissed me back, *milaya moya*," he said softly, feeling the kick of it when her cheeks stained red again, the truth right there, written across her fair skin, his to use against her as he wished.

And that was the problem. *He wished.*

His brows arched high, daring her to deny it. Daring her to lie to him, to his face, when he knew better. "And you liked it."

CHAPTER TWO

FINALLY! Miranda thought in relief as she arrived back at her hotel room in Georgetown much later that evening. *You can drop the act.*

She let the heavy door slam shut behind her, and entertained the notion that she was ill instead of…thrown. But she knew better. She locked the door and then leaned back against it, sliding all the way down to the ground, hugging her knees to her chest and burying her head against them.

She didn't cry. Not quite. She didn't weep over the bruises on her upper arms, or the fact they throbbed slightly now. She thought about how scared she'd been one minute, and then how off balance and confused, if inexplicably safe, the next. She thought about that damned kiss and her wild response, and how little she understood what had happened to her when Ivan Korovin had touched her. She thought about what *out of control* meant, and how unacceptable that was for her. She didn't let out the old, terrified sobs that she'd thought she'd put behind her so long ago, though she could feel them clawing at her throat, insistent at the back of her eyes.

She squeezed her eyes shut tight, she fought for breath, and then she simply sat there and held herself for a very long time. If she sat still long enough, maybe the nightmares wouldn't come this time. Maybe she could think them away. *Maybe.*

She'd made it through the rest of her day on autopilot. She'd taped a segment on school bullying with one cable news channel and had suffered through an early dinner with her literary agent, who was in town to wrangle a loudmouthed politician's ex-wife into a book deal and who had eyed Miranda with what looked like pity when she'd tried to discuss her work.

"The truth is," Bob had said baldly over his filet, "you need to come up with something sexy as a follow-up to *Caveman Worship.* Nothing you've mentioned tonight is sexy."

Which was his obnoxious way of telling her that her publisher had rejected her latest book proposal.

And as she'd sat there at dinner, pretending she found this latest rejection a delightful intellectual challenge instead of another crushing defeat, what had really bothered Miranda was that she hadn't been able to regulate her temperature. Too hot, too cold, like some impossible fever—and she couldn't get Ivan Korovin's frank midnight gaze out of her head. The way he'd *looked* at her, as if she was dessert and he wanted to indulge. Like he'd been imagining doing it right then and there in the conference hotel lobby, no matter what barely civilized things he might have said.

How could one man make her feel safe and out of control at the same time?

Eventually, the worst of the storm passed. She leaned her head back against the door and blew out a long breath. She kicked off her shoes and tied her long hair back into a low ponytail, wishing she'd booked herself on the train back to her home in New York City tonight. She'd planned to sleep in the following morning and then head back to her office on the Columbia University campus, where she'd taught since being awarded her Ph.D. there three years ago, reinvigorated from the conference and plotting out how she'd use what she'd learned in her latest article.

She hadn't planned on that awful Guberev. Much less Ivan Korovin.

Or that devastating mouth of his.

A long, hot bath will do the trick, she told herself now, rubbing her hands over her face, trying to banish all of her ghosts. Old and new. All those nightmares in the making. *Along with a nice big glass of wine.*

This was nothing more than a delayed reaction to Guberev and the sickeningly familiar sensations he had unleashed within her. And all of those memories of her childhood—but that was nothing Miranda particularly wanted to confront head-on tonight.

Unbidden, then, she remembered the way Ivan Korovin, of all people, had pulled her against him. So gently. So easily. He hadn't been what she'd expected, what she'd imagined him to be. What she'd spent a lot of airtime telling people he was. That rich, dark voice, like the finest chocolate, that had seemed to warm her no matter how cold the words he used. That stern, black gaze of his that had seen too much. The way he'd held her, as if she was precious enough to save. As if she really was his. That had been dizzying enough. And then that kiss…

She sank down on the soft bed that took up most of the efficient room—almost involuntarily, as if his kiss was still *that potent* in her memory. She was obviously more shaken up than she'd thought. She remembered that she'd switched her phone off before her segment earlier and pulled her bag to her now, rummaging through the outside pocket. Finding her cell phone, she powered it up and sat there, waiting, flexing her bare, stiff toes into the carpeted floor beneath her and staring out the window into the Georgetown night.

Breathe, she ordered herself. But she couldn't seem to pull in a deep enough breath, and all she could see was that considering gleam in Ivan's midnight gaze. Something licked in her then, dark and secret, and she felt herself flush with an unwelcome heat. She told herself she was over-tired.

She glanced down at her phone as the welcome screen appeared, and watched as the tiny icon noting the number of missed calls appeared.

And rose.

And kept rising.

Next to it, another icon showing her number of emails did the same. Ten. Twenty. Thirty-five. Forty. Her heart began to beat fast and hard, as if to match.

Miranda was still frowning down at the phone

in her hand when the room phone shrilled loudly from the bedside table. She jumped, and that was when she noticed that the red light on the hotel phone was blinking, too, indicating even more messages to go along with the mounting numbers on her cell phone.

Fifty. Sixty-two.

Her heart gave a great thump in her chest. Then again. The hotel phone shrilled insistently. Feeling shaky again, and not sure why or what, exactly, she was afraid of, she forced herself to lean over and snatch it up.

"Hello?"

"Professor."

It was Ivan Korovin, as if she'd conjured him with her wayward thoughts. She flushed hot and hated herself for it, but she would know that voice anywhere. The erotic flavor of his native Russian, that commanding tone that was purely his. It snaked through her, wrapping around her, pulling tight inside and out. She couldn't think of a single reason why this man should be calling her. Something pulsed, hard and hot and deep in her belly, and she hated herself for that, too.

"We have nothing to discuss," she said, proud

of herself for sounding so calm. So in control. She glanced down at her phone and swallowed. Seventy-three. Eighty-nine. What was going on?

"On the contrary," he said, and the tone he used then made her realize somewhat belatedly that there were layers of steel to him, ruthlessness and authority, that he'd been holding in reserve before.

"We have a great deal to discuss," he continued in the kind of tone that suggested he expected nothing less than swift and immediate obedience, from her and anyone else hapless enough to stumble into his path. Hadn't he spoken in much the same tone to Guberev? "My car is waiting for you downstairs."

"I can't imagine what would make you think I'd go anywhere with you," she said almost conversationally, as if she didn't feel the obviously insane urge to simply do what he wanted, no questions asked. But she knew where that sort of blind obedience led, didn't she? Nowhere a smart woman wanted to go. And she had no idea what had happened to her today, what she'd become when he'd touched her—what he'd made her with that kiss that still seemed to ricochet through her body, sending up showers of sparks even all these hours later—but she had always prided herself on being smart. It had saved her once before. It would now. It was her greatest— and only—weapon. "Frankly, I don't think I've heard a more spectacularly bad idea."

There was a short, loaded pause. She could almost *see* that dark, fulminating gaze of his, could imagine it running over her skin like heat. She despaired of herself as her body reacted, readying itself for a possession she had no intention of allowing.

"I take it you have not checked your messages, then?"

Her heart seemed to explode against her ribs. She even looked wildly around the room in a panic, as if she thought he might leap out from behind the drapes.

But she was alone. And he, apparently, was psychic.

"How do you know I have messages?" she demanded, and she was too thrown to care that she sounded as unnerved as she felt. That her voice actually shook, and he could undoubtedly hear it as well as she could.

"Listen to a few of them." It was another command, and harsher this time. Her heart was still pounding too hard for her to protest. "Then I suggest you get in the car."

"You play a dangerous game, brother."

Ivan did not have to look up from the screen of his laptop to identify the voice speaking in Russian from the doorway. He knew it as well as his own.

"Guberev?" he asked as his brother Nikolai came to stand behind him.

"Handled. He won't be an issue again." Ivan could sense Nikolai's cold smile then; he didn't have to turn to see it. "He promised me personally, and you know how I feel about promises."

For a moment, they both watched the screen on the coffee table. It was an old video of Professor Miranda Sweet on one of those interchangeable American gossip programs, talking. Always talking. And Ivan was her favorite subject.

"Ivan Korovin is a man, not a myth," she was saying, so cool and composed, looking unassailable and far too *correct*. It made him want to reach through the screen and mess her up, somehow. With his hands. His mouth. It made him want to take her on a tour of the terrible things he'd lived through, the things he'd done and had done to him, that she cheapened, somehow, with these attacks. "We tell ourselves his treatment of women in the Jonas Dark films is just part of the character he plays, but then we breathlessly follow his questionable exploits with Hollywood starlets as if it's some kind of extended reel of those same films—"

Ivan reached out and clicked the pause button, then picked up his drink and swirled it around in the heavy crystal tumbler. Sometimes he wondered, in the darkest places inside of him, if it were true. If she was right. If she saw something in him he'd thought he'd excised from himself when he was still young. If he was a brutal pig of a man like the uncle who had raised him—all drunken fists and unrestrained savagery. Even if he'd spent the whole of his adult life distancing himself from men like that.

No doubt that was the reason he'd concocted this little plan to destroy her. At last.

He owed her nothing less. She wasn't merely his most vocal enemy, so quick to tear him down in public. That would have been bad enough. But Professor Miranda Sweet made him question *who he was*. She made him doubt himself, when he was the only thing he'd ever had to depend upon. It was unforgivable.

And he wanted her, finally, to pay. That kiss might have been a mistake, but the opportunities it had presented to him once he had time to think, to strategize, felt far more like fate.

"This is begging for trouble," Nikolai said, walking around to the front of the sofa and fixing Ivan with that frigid glare of his. "You are far too fascinated with a woman you need only to seduce and then discard."

Ivan knew, intellectually, that his brother was a threat. His years as a soldier, the things he'd done, all he'd lost—these things made him dangerous. Unpredictable and lethal. A hard, damaged man. But he still saw only his younger brother when he looked at him. And his own guilt.

He shrugged as if he was unconcerned. "Surely the fascination will only help in the seduction."

Nikolai's cold eyes moved over Ivan's face. "There are some fights even you can't win, Vanya."

He used the old nickname that Ivan only tolerated from family—and Nikolai was the only one left. Ivan eyed his younger brother appraisingly. Nikolai had not answered to his own family nickname in many years now. His demons were so much closer to the surface, raw and hungry. They always had been. Ivan's tended to lurk deeper, and bite down harder. He could feel their teeth in his flesh, digging deep, even now.

"Your faith in me is touching," Ivan said after a moment, trying not to step on his brother's many land mines, scattered all around them. He could almost see them with his own eyes and, as ever, felt nothing but the same old guilt for his part in setting them in the first place.

"There are so many who believe that Hollywood mask of yours," Nikolai said. "But I know you. I know she makes you bleed, little though you might show it."

Ivan sighed. "You think I will be bested by a woman who is all bark and no bite, Nikolai? Have I fallen so far?"

"That is not the fight that worries me," Nikolai said in a low voice, his shadowed gaze clashing with Ivan's. He jerked his chin at the computer screen, his mouth flattening. "You should not want what you cannot have."

Nikolai refused to talk about it, so Ivan no longer asked about the wife who had left Nikolai some five years ago and taken what scant hap-

piness his brother had ever known with her—
what little happiness that might have been left
after all his harsh years in the Russian special
forces. Now Nikolai prided himself on being a
stripped-down, shut-off machine who wanted
almost nothing.

For this, too, Ivan blamed only himself.

On the laptop screen, the professor was frozen
in place, her mouth deceptively soft, her delicate
hands framing some point in midair. And Ivan
knew, now, how she tasted—how she felt against
him. He knew exactly how he'd make her pay for
the things she'd said about him. All the deals he
might have lost because of her campaign against
him, the potential donors who balked at the idea
of giving money to a man better known as a barbarian than a philanthropist, all thanks to her.

He told himself that would make the revenge
he took all the sweeter.

"There are many ways to want," he said now,
quietly.

Nikolai snorted. "And far more ways than that
to lose."

"You don't need to worry about me, Nikolai,"
he said gruffly. "I know what I'm doing."

But he was more than a little afraid that he was
a liar.

* * *

Ivan Korovin, naturally, was staying in a palatial suite in the nicest hotel in Georgetown, far from the bustle and clamor of the conference. Miranda strode confidently across the lobby and into the private elevator that led to the penthouse suite, where she leaned against the wall and would have crumpled in on herself a little bit if she hadn't been aware of the cameras, no doubt recording her every move. Anyone could be watching. Even him. The thought of his brooding black gaze on her, when she couldn't see him in return, kept her defiantly upright.

The elevator doors opened smoothly and delivered her into a private, gilt-edged foyer, dizzy with frescoed walls and marble floors. Miranda stepped out into it, her heels loud against the hard floor, and then froze as the doors slid shut behind her. Flashes from earlier in the day scorched through her. Ivan's hands. His mouth. That *look*.

Why are you really *here?* a small, suspicious voice asked inside of her, and she didn't have an answer. Not one she liked.

She reached out as if to call back the elevator, but the great door at the other end of the foyer opened then, and it was too late. A terrifying man with a face like a honed and deadly blade glared at her, and she swallowed. His eyes were the harshest, coldest blue she'd ever seen, and burned like ice against her skin. But she somehow kept herself from stepping back, or showing any of the nerves that made her knees feel a little bit too weak beneath her.

"My name is Miranda—"

"Yes," he said, cutting her off coldly, in another Russian-accented voice, though this one was a great deal less like chocolate and far more like a Cyrillic-infused knife, straight to her jugular. "We know who you are. We would not have let you up in the elevator if we did not."

He led her through the overwhelmingly grand suite, his disapproval as obvious as it was silent. Miranda became more nervous with every step. She shouldn't have come here. What could Ivan Korovin possibly have to say that was worth subjecting herself to this? But she followed as expected, and eventually she was ushered into a cozy, quiet sitting area that featured pretty views over the city through huge, ostentatiously curtained windows.

Ivan stood there, his strong back to her, far more impressive than his luxurious surroundings. The imposing security guard disappeared, closing the door behind him. Ivan seemed bigger here than in her memory. More intimidating, somehow—or perhaps it was only that she knew, now, how very dangerous he really was. *To her.* It was no longer an academic exercise. It was distressingly personal. And even so, as she had earlier today, she immediately felt something ease in her when she saw him.

Safe, that voice whispered inside of her. She couldn't understand it. Surely he was the most dangerous of all? Surely this entire day had proved that?

He turned to meet her gaze, his own that deep, mesmerizing midnight, and a dark current seemed to hum too loud in her, drowning out her confusion. Then a devastating pulse of awareness reverberated down her spine and sent out shock waves as he closed the distance between them and beckoned her toward one of the elegant gold-and-cream sofas with a wave of his hand. He moved like liquid, ruthless and sure. He was a nightmare made real, and she couldn't understand why her body didn't seem to know it.

She ignored the invitation to sit. She called it self-preservation.

"Why does a man like you need bodyguards?" she asked, not aware she meant to speak.

His dark brows arched high. "By 'a man like me,' do I assume you mean rich? Famous?"

"Deadly," she replied. She fought to control her own expression when his hardened, when he seemed to move closer to her without having moved at all. "Shouldn't a man with your particular skills be able to handle himself?"

"Most lunatics use guns," he said with a certain calm resignation that sent a chill spiraling through her. "And fists are somewhat inadequate from certain distances, I find. But I appreciate your interest in my security arrangements, Dr. Sweet. I'm sure it is benevolent."

She didn't like how he said her name. Or, if she was brutally honest, she didn't like how very much she did like it—he said it as if he was tasting it with that wicked mouth of his. But she wasn't here to sink any further into that mire. She couldn't. How had she wandered off on this tangent when there was so much to discuss—and all of it far more important that his damned mouth?

But even as she thought about that mouth, it seemed to relent. "And in any case, that was my brother."

"Your brother?" Although now that she thought about it, the other man had been like a far colder, far more terrifying Ivan, hadn't he? It boggled the mind.

"Nikolai acts as my bodyguard when he feels it necessary," Ivan said. His dark brows rose. "Would you like me to explain to you the peculiar swamp of Korovin family dynamics? Would that make you feel more at ease? You look as if you are about to faint."

"I'm fine," she snapped. And then couldn't contain what was swirling inside of her another second. "This is a complete disaster, and it's your fault. I told you it would affect my career and I was right. And that was before we made the news!"

The kiss had gone viral. Every person Miranda had ever met, it seemed, had called or e-mailed or texted to inform her that they'd seen the clip of it. Online or e-mailed to them. Then on television. Of Ivan's hands all over her and her seemingly enthusiastic acceptance of it and, worse, her response to it. To him.

I am a very possessive man, he'd told her in that dark, stirring voice of his, picked up by all those cameras. He'd looked down at her as if she was edible and he was starving. She'd watched it herself on her own laptop in her hotel room. Over and over. She'd watched him kiss her so thoroughly, almost lazily, as if he had all the time in the world and every right. With such raw, carnal power that she'd felt it explode inside of her all over again. She'd watched herself simply...submit. Surrender. And then melt all over him like wax against a flame.

There was no way she could lie to herself about what had happened, about how she'd responded to him. It had been right there in front of her. He'd been the one to kiss her and he'd been the one to pull back when he was done, but she'd been the one draped against him, boneless and glassy-eyed and evidently mindless.

Opposites Really Do Attract! the online gossip sites had shrieked. *Mortal Enemies in Not-So-Mortal Combat? Korovin's Kiss KOs the Competition!*

Ivan Korovin is sexy with a capital *S*! her agent had texted while she was obediently sitting in the back of Ivan's chauffeured car, too upset with the situation to be as outraged as she should have been at his high-handedness. He's a bestseller on two feet!

Clearly, Ivan Korovin kissing anyone with a pulse would be a story. She'd seen that story a thousand times herself—Ivan with this model or that starlet. She'd discussed that story in detail, dissecting the dramatic tales his various women always told in the wake of their affairs with him. But Ivan Korovin kissing the starchy professor best known for calling him "a barbaric King Leonidas without the excuse of a Sparta"? Miranda didn't need her agent to tell her how salacious *that* story was.

"It seems we are thrown together in this, like it or not," Ivan said then, breaking her out of the dark spiral of her thoughts with his far darker, far richer voice. "Perhaps it would be better if we tried to think of it as an opportunity."

He was dressed in casual black trousers slung low on his narrow hips and a soft, charcoal-gray T-shirt that strained over his rock-hard biceps and clung to his well-honed gladiatorial torso. A darkly inked tattoo in an intricate pattern wrapped around the tight muscles of his left upper arm, twisting around to end just above his wrist. His thick, dark hair was damp, which felt like a kind of unearned, unwanted intimacy. It made her imagine him in the shower. It was almost too much to bear.

Even doing no more than simply standing there, he looked distractingly, aggressively male, powerfully masculine, like some kind of potent, lethal work of art. She felt the force of it—of him—as if his very presence a few feet away was the same as his mouth on hers, tutoring her in all those layers of fire and need she'd never imagined existed.

He looked like the warrior he was. She should have been actively repelled by him, and she couldn't understand why she wasn't. Why she still felt as if this untamed, uncivilized menace of a man was *safe* even when he very clearly, very obviously wasn't.

"An opportunity to do what?" she asked, her voice thicker than it should have been. She saw his eyes narrow, and knew he'd noticed it. She crossed her arms as if to ward him off. "Celebrate the end of my career? Who on earth will take me seriously now that I've been seen in such a compromising position with the poster boy for all things violent?"

There was a long, simmering silence. He only looked at her, his dark eyes seeming even blacker than before, his hard face with its much-broken nose forbidding in the soft light of the sitting room lamps. Miranda found it hard to swallow, suddenly, and even harder to breathe, and she was forced to remind herself that he was a very, very dangerous man. A violent man. By trade and training. Possibly also by inclination.

These were all things that should have been foremost in her mind.

"I make action movies," he said in a cold, distinctly hostile tone. There was no sign of temper on that ruthless face of his, which somehow made the lash of it all the worse. "I also practice sambo, among other martial arts, like the rest of my countrymen. It is our national sport. If that makes me the poster boy for all things violent, Professor, I would suggest to you that it's your poster. You're the one who's made me into a monster. I am only a man."

She felt something course through her then that was too close to guilt, to the sickening heat of shame, and she didn't understand it. She didn't want to understand it, just as she didn't want to feel that betraying flood of heat behind her eyes. She didn't want to think about her work from his perspective. She liked the box she'd put him in all these years. She shoved it all aside, and tried to focus on the *point* of this. The reason she was here—and it wasn't to let him take her down in his inimitable way. Again.

"Exactly what opportunities do you see in this mess?" she asked instead, fighting to keep her voice level.

He watched her for another long, intense moment, and Miranda had to order herself not to fidget as she stood there before him. A wild panic surged through her then, alarm bells tolling out a frantic melody, her stomach in a twist, because she had the terrible feeling that whatever was about to happen would ruin her forever, far more comprehensively and irrevocably than any kiss had done. *She knew it.* She could feel it hanging there in the air between them.

And worse, she suspected he knew it, too. As if this was all just one more nightmare waiting to happen, and she the fool who had walked right into it.

Don't be ridiculous! she snapped at herself. Why was she reduced to hysteria in the presence of this man? Miranda had always prided herself on her calm reason, her logic. She'd studied so hard, and from such a young age, to be a scholar—to save herself from moments like this one by thinking her way out of them.

She had weapons, too. She needed to remember that.

But even as she hastily tried to arm herself, his midnight eyes only seemed darker, that temptation of a mouth something near enough to stern, and she had to fight to restrain a shiver. Anticipation or anxiety? She honestly didn't know. His mouth curved, though it was not a smile, not at all, and it danced through her all the same.

"I think we should date," he said.

CHAPTER THREE

"*DATE?*"

She repeated the word in obvious horror, and then again, as if the idea of dating him was profoundly, soul-rendingly disgusting to her.

Ivan imagined that to someone like Miranda Sweet, who he had made it his business to know had been raised in a leafy green American Dream suburb redolent with affluence, it was. She was all Ivy League ivory towers, impressive vocabulary words, intellectual pursuits—the kind of plump, thoughtful life that one could achieve only if one had never wanted for anything. While he had fought his way out of Nizhny Novgorod after the collapse of the Soviet Union with his bare hands and nothing else, save his determination to do anything—absolutely anything—to survive and escape.

Of course she found him disgusting. It was almost amusing, really.

Almost.

That intriguing mouth of hers opened and then closed, and he found himself remembering the heat of it, the intoxicating kick he couldn't seem to shake from his head. Or from the rest of him. Given how unimpressed she was with him, famously so, he should not find her so attractive. He hated that he did—hated even more that Nikolai had noted it. He suspected it spoke to the kind of deep, unmendable flaws that he'd thought he'd fought his way away from, literally, years before.

But then again, when had he ever wanted anything safe? Safety would have been staying in Nizhny Novgorod with his brutal uncle, eking out a living as best he could when the Soviet Union fell all around them. Safety would have been doing something other than fighting. Anything else. No one fought the way he had unless they'd had to; he knew that. He'd lived it. And he had never been anything like safe in all of his life. He wouldn't know how to want such a thing.

But he knew what he was good at: winning. And this particular fight would take logic first, then seduction. The very underhandedness she'd accused him of—because why not live down to her expectations? Why not present her with the very Ivan Korovin she'd been conjuring up on her own all this time? It was only that *fascination* of his that might trip him up.

"I should have realized," she said eventually, her voice cool, though her eyes were much darker than before, hinting at some deeper emotion Ivan could only guess at, and damn her, but he wanted to guess more than he should, "that you're completely insane."

"Not at all," he said. He made no further attempt to conceal his temper, and saw her eyes widen slightly at his tone. "What I am is a businessman. And whatever your opinion of my business, I happen to be extremely good at it. You can't pay for the kind of exposure and reach that today's kiss brought us. My people think, and I agree, that we'd be foolish not to capitalize on it."

But Miranda was shaking her head.

"I don't have the slightest idea what you're talking about," she said in that upper-crust voice of hers that intrigued him as much as it slapped at him.

Ivan felt something twist inside of him. He knew what women like her wanted, and it wasn't a rough, unpedigreed Russian with big fists, no matter how famous he might have become. It was always the same. They wanted the smooth,

polished movie star who only pretended to be a
tough guy. They wanted the magazine spreads
and the glossy premieres. They never wanted any
of the darkness beneath, the things he'd done or
the places he'd been—and, in fact, usually bolted
at the first sight of it.

"If you would condescend to sit down, Professor," he said, unable to keep the edge from his
voice, "I would be happy to explain it to you."

As expected, she looked at him as if she thought
he was some kind of wild dog, howling into the
night. She settled herself primly on the edge of
the nearest sofa, her back straight, her dark red
hair in a long, silken tail down her back. Everything about her deliberate, careful posture, he
realized as he threw himself on the sofa opposite her, irritated him. Made him feel too big, too
wild, too dangerous. Too dirty, too beneath her.
Too much.

Oh, yes, he thought. She'd pay.

"Are you trying to provoke me?" His voice
was hard, cracking across the lavish table that
slouched between them, glass and gold and a riot
of fresh flowers in the center. "Is that why you're
acting as if you've been thrown into a lion's den?"

"I have been," she replied, her eyes gleaming

green with the temper that didn't—quite—sound in her voice. "Who knows what you might do next? You introduced yourself mouth-first."

"Are you claiming what you feel right now is fear?" he asked, almost amused again. Or so he told himself.

She only glared back at him, clearly unaware that he found her defiance impossibly sexy. He had no intention of sharing that with her. Women like this one already had far too many weapons at their disposal. Why should he hand her another?

"Your pulse is racing," he told her softly, as sure of this, of her, as he would have been about any opponent in any ring. He hadn't lied when he'd told her he was good at what he did. "And your skin is flushed. Your pupils are slightly dilated and you keep worrying your lower lip with your teeth. That is not fear. It is attraction."

For a moment she stared at him, aghast. And then Ivan saw that *something else* move beneath it, that simmering fire that was causing all of this trouble in the first place.

"You don't know me well enough to make that determination." But her voice was far too constricted and she sat even straighter, if possible, and pressed her soft lips into a tight line.

He wanted to lick her all over, starting there.

"I don't need to know you at all." He shrugged. "I know people, and I know how to read physical tells."

She scowled at him. "What do physical tells have to do with anything?" Her hands tightened on her lap, as if she wanted to clench them into fists, but thought better of it at the last moment. "The physical is the least important part of attraction. It's nothing but smoke and mirrors. The brain is what really matters."

He really was amused. Finally. He leaned back against the sofa. "Then, Professor, I am sorry to tell you this, but you're doing it wrong."

She was so much prettier in person, he thought then, even as she glared at him in all of her high-class fury. He was so much more susceptible to her than he'd ever dreamed he'd be. *Damn her.* It made everything that much more complicated. Or it made him a fool. He supposed it was the same result either way.

She tensed as if she was debating running for the door. But she only breathed for a moment, then relaxed again, however slightly, and he wished he knew why. He wished he could read whatever was going on behind that smooth, compelling triangle of her face. *He wished*, and he was old enough, battle-scarred enough, to know better.

"Is that why you think we should date?" she asked then, her tone crisp with disbelief. And all those other things he wanted far too much to uncover and identify, one by one. "So you can regale me with your theories about the physiological reactions of total strangers?"

"That would be a side benefit, of course."

"This is ridiculous," she said, standing then, practically vibrating with tension. Or was it something else? He had the sudden sense that she was far more emotional, perhaps even fragile, than he'd imagined. Than she showed. But he didn't want to think of her that way. "I knew I shouldn't have come here. My life is disintegrating around me and your solution is to *date*?"

"Calm yourself, please." He stretched his legs out in front of him as if he had never been more at ease, enjoying the way her dark eyes narrowed in outrage. It was better than the possibility of tears, however remote. "It obviously wouldn't be a real relationship. I am well aware of your opinion of me. I am no fonder of you. In that sense, we are perfectly matched."

Which was true, of course. But it did not address this *thing* between them that had nearly burned him alive where he stood earlier. And Ivan only had to look at her to know that bringing up the best way he knew of to deal with that kind of wildfire, out-of-control chemistry—in the nearest bed, for a week or so—would only cloud the issue unnecessarily. Not to mention, force her to vehemently deny something that he had every intention of proving to his satisfaction. At length.

But not now.

"Why would you even suggest something like this? Is that how people do things in Hollywood?" She looked scandalized. "I didn't think that was true. Not really."

"Surely you cannot deny the power of that kiss," he said, for no other reason than to poke at her. Or so he told himself. He shrugged languidly when she stiffened. "If you can, you are alone. Last I checked, the clip has been watched in excess of—"

"There is no accounting for taste," she blurted, as if she couldn't bear to think about how many people had seen the video. Seen them. The perfect Ivy League professor with a shined-up Russian thug all over her. She no doubt felt contaminated by his very public touch. Forever marred. It made him want only to dirty her further. Here. Now.

"Indeed." He eyed her. Forced his voice to remain cool. "Just as there is no denying our on-screen chemistry. Think of the headlines we could generate if we actually tried."

"You have to be kidding me—" she began, though he could see the heat across her cheeks, telling him far more than her words ever could. For one thing, that she wanted him just as much as he wanted her, however loath she was to admit it.

He could use that. He would.

"I am changing careers." He watched her process that. That blink. That considering tilt of her head. Why should he find such things so powerfully compelling? "Again."

"Racing about the world claiming that unnecessary kisses are a new form of chivalry?" she asked drily. It was as if she couldn't help herself. "With your fame and fans, I'm sure you could turn it into quite the cottage industry. A moveable kissing booth, if you will. Headlines and chemistry at every turn, just the way you like it."

"Philanthropy," he replied, and watched her redden further, as if he'd chastised her. "My last

Jonas Dark movie comes out in June. My new
charity will be kicking off with its first major
event a week or so later. It can only benefit me,
as I make the switch from action hero to philanthropist, to have my most outspoken critic show
the world she sees me as a man, not merely the
Neanderthal fighting machine she has claimed I
am on every available media outlet for the past
two years."

That had been the main thrust of his publicist's
argument earlier, as Ivan had watched the clip of
the kiss on one of the major gossip programs in
disbelief. Ivan had been unable to get his head
around the fact that he was now linked to his
nemesis in this way. And worse, that he had no
one to blame for his predicament but himself.
That last had been Nikolai's main point—that
and the suggestion that he take this opportunity
to neutralize the Miranda Sweet issue once and
for all.

Why had he kissed her?

But Ivan was nothing if not practical. No matter the force of his *fascinations*. No matter what
price he might have to pay. And so there was no
reason he couldn't make this little game work
for him on a number of levels, he thought as he

watched her now, that dark shimmer of red in her hair, that lush mouth, that unconscious patrician *certainty* of hers. No reason in the world.

The plan had practically made itself. Revenge might have been a dish better served cold, but that wasn't to say it wasn't just as effective hot and wild. He supposed he'd find out.

"I can see how that would benefit *you*," she said after a moment, her tone suggesting he had begged for her help on his knees—as if he needed her desperately and she was trying her hardest to be polite in the face of such naked entreaty. He bit back a laugh at the image.

"Let's not get carried away." His voice was dry, no hint of the laughter that moved in him. "I said that it could benefit me, not that I needed it. I don't. But I could use you, certainly."

"I appreciate the distinction," she said in that cool way that made him ache to find his way into the fire she hid beneath it. "But I can't quite see how going along with this would do anything for me but make me a hypocrite."

"Please." He did not precisely scoff at her. He didn't have to. "I'm a movie star. There's no way you could ever generate this kind of exposure on your own. We'll play to the public's obvious fas-

cination with the possibility that so appalls you—
that a man like me and a woman like you could
ever be together. They'll eat it up. We'll break up
after about a month or so, milk the rumors and
go our merry ways. I don't see the downside."

"Because there isn't one," she said quietly,
something that looked much darker than simple
panic in the green of her gaze. "*For you.* It actually matters to me that people will see me as a
hypocrite. That, in fact, I'll *be* a hypocrite." She
made a low noise. "Not everything is for sale."

"Spoken by someone who never had to sell
something precious in order to stay alive."

He couldn't hide his impatience—nor his irri-
tation at her and all the people like her, who had
been born rich and privileged and would never
know what it was like to have to choose between
their pride and their survival. Much less fight for
it with their own hands. Much less lose so much
of themselves, and everything else that mattered,
along the way.

"I understand you, too, Professor," he told her,
his own voice much colder than it had been.
"You're not the only one who studies their opponents. I know precisely what kind of princess
you like to pretend you never were."

Her eyes flew to his, stricken, and that delicious color rose in her cheeks again, making him feel the same kind of rush he'd felt in the ring when he'd won a tough round. He supposed that confirmed that he was exactly the Neanderthal she believed he was, and in that moment he didn't care.

"That seems like an ineffective bargaining tool," she said after a short pause, and while he could hear that he'd got to her in the scratchiness in her voice, see it in that extra bright sheen to her dark jade eyes, she still said it calmly. Coolly. As if she was utterly unfazed. He felt a trickle of reluctant admiration work through him. "Bludgeoning someone you're trying to persuade with a highly slanted interpretation of their biography. Not the smoothest approach, I'd have thought."

"Try this one," he suggested. "Guberev actually is the animal you would like to think I am." It shouldn't bother him in the slightest to lie to her, to manipulate the fear he'd seen she felt. It was one more strategy, wasn't it? All worth it in the end, no matter how it felt now. No matter that it made him who she thought he was. "I don't know what he wanted from you, but the fact that he felt comfortable showing up at a summit and approaching you in the way he did should give you pause."

"It does."

"Then I offer you, again, the perfect solution to make sure he keeps his distance from you."

"Because he is like a dog who responds to shows of domination, is that it?" she asked. "Does that make you the alpha in this scenario?"

Her smile was wintry then, and he should not have felt it like a touch. He should not have wanted to lick into it, beneath it, to taste her again. He should not have been contemplating the best way to get under her too-privileged skin. He should not have been so conflicted about what he was doing here. He should not have worried if his brother was right, after all—that there were too many ways to lose, and he was courting every one of them.

Miranda's cold smile only deepened, as if she could read him, too. "Because if so, I'm afraid I know exactly what it makes me," she said.

The room seemed to stretch tight around them, and Miranda couldn't remember the last time she'd taken a full breath. No wonder she felt so off balance.

It wasn't only that he'd called her a *princess* in that insulting way, as if she was some kind of socialite. It wasn't only that he wanted to *date* her, of all things—but only as an elaborate ruse. It wasn't the *fact* of him, so big and male and inarguably powerful, sitting there so close to her, like he was waiting to pounce. She concentrated on filling her lungs. In. Out. It was the only thing she was sure she could control.

Ivan started to speak again, but she threw up one of her hands, palm out, and stopped him, happy to see that for some reason, her hand wasn't shaking the way she was afraid the rest of her was. Or soon would.

"I'm going to have to think about all of this," she said, and she hated that there was a part of her that sounded almost *pleading*, as if, by walking into this hotel suite tonight, she had handed over her right to make decisions about her own life. "I'll get back to you—"

"That is impossible," he said, cutting her off. When she frowned at him, he only shrugged in that languid, lazy way of his that she was quickly coming to loathe. "We either use the momentum of this kiss to our benefit now, or we wait for it to blow over. For me, that will be very soon.

For you? Perhaps not." His hard mouth curved faintly. He was daring her, she realized, as her skin seemed to pull tight in response. "I wonder, are you more of a hypocrite if you are seen to date me, this man that you so famously hate— or if, having kissed me in so wanton a fashion in front of all the world, you don't?"

That question hung there between them. Miranda became aware of the rushing sound in her ears and the rapid clamor of her pulse, just as he'd pointed out before. And that too-tight feeling all over, like her skin was too small for her body. She forced herself to ignore it. And to *think*.

The fact was, she knew he was on to something, however far-fetched and insane it sounded. However trapped she felt. She knew that a few accusations of hypocrisy were nothing compared to the kind of notoriety "dating" him would grant her—and notoriety would not only sell book proposals and the books that came from them, but guarantee that her presence as a pundit, as the go-to sound bite, was assured. As her agent had told her already, Ivan Korovin was sexy. The entire world was obsessed with him. If she went along with this, she would build her profile to unimaginable heights and would then be that much more able to get her message out, which was all she'd ever wanted in the first place. How could she turn that down and still live with herself?

Besides, she thought, letting her gaze sweep over him, he really was the ultimate modern warrior. The biggest and the baddest of all the swaggering fighter types who dreamed of being just like him. These days he dominated the box office the same way he'd dominated the ring, and she'd seen for herself that he was even more formidable in person.

"Dating" him would be like taking a trip through the belly of the beast. It would be taking her research to a previously unimagined level: testing her theories at the source. Interviewing the monster he'd claimed she'd made him in his very own lair.

She sat back down on the sofa opposite him gingerly, crossing her legs, and smoothed her hands down the front of her trousers. She could feel his eyes on her, black and hooded, as he waited with a watchful patience that seemed like another kind of caress, and just as dangerous. She told herself it was only the enormity—and inarguable insanity—of what she was about to do that made her hands feel faintly damp against her legs.

Excitement, she assured herself, *not anxiety. And excitement for the book possibilities here, the career boost—not for him!*

But she knew she was a liar when she met his gaze and felt it sear straight through her, down to the soles of her feet, kicking up all of that heat and longing and fire along the way.

That could only bode ill. She knew that, too.

She was going to do it anyway.

"I want to write a book," she told him, and as she said it, she saw it all flash before her, as if it was preordained. She could call it something like *Caveman Confidential*. Her publisher would eat it up, and the public would rush out in droves to buy it, so desperate were they for this man. Even if what she said about him was negative. Ivan looked blank. She smiled. "About you."

"Out of the question." He didn't even pretend to consider it. "I do very minimal press, and no biographies. Ever."

"Yes, I know." Miranda bit back a sigh and schooled her expression into something that might pass for detached. Unmoved. *Uninvested.* "You refuse to talk about your past. You refuse to discuss your personal life. You refuse, and because of that, you're everybody's favorite mystery. Well, if I'm going to risk my reputation, you can't refuse me. I want total access."

"Why would I grant such a thing to someone who has already built her so-called career on tearing me to pieces in the public eye?" he asked with soft yet unmistakable menace. "Why would I give you ammunition?"

Miranda didn't much care for the so-called-career comment, but she also didn't mistake the steel in his tone. It would not do to forget who and what this man was. What he could do.

"You cannot possibly think me that much of a fool, Professor. Can you?"

"Consider it your chance," she said, her mind racing.

"My chance to do what?" he asked drily. "Deliver myself willingly into your tender claws?"

"To prove me wrong."

He let his gaze drag over her. Her mouth, her neck. Her breasts. Lower. It was deliberate. Obvious. And even so, she felt the heat of it. The kick.

"I have had more appealing offers." He was so arrogant. Every inch the wealthy, famous man. It set her teeth on edge, but she pushed on.

"Then think of it as a challenge." She raised her brows when his midnight gaze met hers again. "Convince me that I'm wrong about you. Convince me that I've been wrong about you all along. Isn't that what you think?"

"It is what I know. It is also true."

The way he said that seemed to hum in her. Like foreboding. Miranda shoved the feeling aside. She wanted this, suddenly, as if she'd come up with the idea herself. She wanted it *fiercely.*

"Show me," she said quietly, terrified he could hear how much she wanted him to agree in her voice. Terrified he was perverse enough to do precisely the opposite because of it. "Everything. And I'll pretend to date you. I'll do whatever you want."

Ages could have passed then, as he regarded her calmly from across the table in that unnerving way of his, those dark eyes of his missing nothing. He only lounged there, looking as if he was lazily mulling over what she'd said—but Miranda knew better now. There was nothing lazy about him. He was like a snake poised to strike, and twice as deadly.

"There will be rules," he said after a while, his gaze intent on hers. "If you break them, no book.

For example, if you find you cannot handle the attention we'll get? No book."

"Fine." She hardly dared breathe. Was he really going to do this? Let her this close to him? Tell her things he'd steadfastly refused to tell anyone else? Let her shape it how she wished? She couldn't believe it. "I have rules, too."

"Of course." He ran his fingers over his mouth, and it tugged at her as if it was her mouth he was touching in exactly the same way. "Such as?"

"No touching unless there are cameras around," she said. Too fast. Much too fast. His black eyes shone with a dark amusement. "There have to be boundaries."

"That is your first concern?" He sounded entirely too pleased. "Not what I think the role will entail? Not what it is like to live life in so many flashbulbs? Not what we will do if this game of pretend shifts into something else entirely?" That hard curve that flirted with a smile was mesmerizing. "Interesting."

"Don't psychoanalyze me," she said, meaning to snap at him, but it came out much softer. Too much softer. As she was already losing herself, before the game had even begun. "And there will be no *shifting*."

"Is that another rule?"

"A very strong preference."

"Let me tell you my most important preference," he said in that smoke-and-chocolate voice, and if she hadn't known better, if she hadn't been sitting there unable to look away from him, she would have thought he was touching her. Running his hands all over her. Making her his that easily. "I like to be in charge. Accept that and this will be far easier for you."

She could imagine it, then. Him. All of that wildness and darkness and fire. In vivid color. She who had always thought of sex in muted tones, pleasant pastels…what was he doing to her? She knew better than to let the nightmares in. To *invite* them.

"You can be in charge of our fake relationship all you like," she said, her voice betraying her, too husky and too warm. Filled with all the things she didn't want to admit were in her head, and leaving shivery trails all through her body. "Just so long as you answer my questions. *All* my questions. No stonewalling. No diversions. You have to give me what I want, or I walk. That's the only deal I'm prepared to make."

She thought she sounded tough. Cool. Competent. Nothing more than a dedicated researcher, outlining her terms.

"As you wish, Professor," he said then.

He did not sound in the least compliant. His dark eyes shone with a potent mixture of amusement and triumph, hard and hot. It connected with her belly, her breath.

"Okay," she said, while her heart did cartwheels in her chest and she couldn't seem to tear her gaze away from him, no matter what. "Then I guess we have a deal."

Ivan's black eyes blazed.

And Miranda was left with the unsettling notion that she'd done exactly what he'd expected her to do. That he'd led her straight here and she'd walked directly into his trap.

As if he'd known precisely what she would do, what she would say, when she'd come to him tonight.

As if he'd planned it.

CHAPTER FOUR

IVAN insisted on starting this game of theirs immediately. And in Paris.

"That is unacceptable," he'd told her that first night in Washington when Miranda had protested that she could simply meet him in a few days in Cannes, where, they'd agreed, they would use the annual film festival as an opportunity to show off their brand-new fake relationship. "We will go to Europe together, of course."

He'd dismissed her protest with a certain casual ease and expectation of instant obedience that had knotted her stomach. Miranda had not cared for the uneasiness that had moved through her then, whispering suspicions she'd been afraid to look at too closely. What had she gotten herself into with this man? But she'd been afraid she knew.

"What do you plan to wear on the red carpet?" he'd asked in the same tone. He'd waved a hand dismissively over the tailored black trouser suit she wore that until that moment she'd thought was both professional and pretty. "This?"

Miranda had refused to curl up in humiliation, as she'd been fairly certain he'd intended she do. She'd wondered if that was what he was really after—if this was his revenge, to strip her down and try to embarrass her. If so, she'd thought, eyeing him across the coffee table, refusing to cower, he was in for a surprise. She'd survived far worse than this. She would survive him, too.

"I own dresses, thank you," she'd informed him. Through her teeth. "I've even attended fancy events before, believe it or not."

"This is not a negotiation, Professor," Ivan had replied, still lounging there on that cream-and-gold sofa in that ostentatious hotel suite. His voice had been firm. "I have a reputation to uphold. A woman who appears on my arm must live up to certain expectations, a certain standard. We are not talking about a cocktail party filled with self-satisfied academics at your university or uppity Greenwich, Connecticut, yacht club members—we are talking about the world stage."

She'd reminded herself then that she'd already hated him on principle alone for years, so it wasn't as if there had been any further to fall.

"And on this world stage of yours, fashion is everything?" she'd asked, unable to keep the derision from her tone and not, she'd admitted to herself, trying too hard.

He'd only watched her, those impossibly dark eyes seeing far too much, brooding and amused at once.

"On my particular stage," he'd replied, not quite mocking her, not quite putting her in whatever he thought her place was, she'd decided; *not quite*, "fashion is a statement of intent. A declaration of purpose. It is taken very seriously, like it or not."

"Fine," she'd said stiffly. She'd reminded herself of her greater goals, the plans she'd been so eager to put into action. The book she would write, exposing him, that would make all of these humiliations, large and small, worthwhile. That would allow her to continue reaching out to those, like her, who were tired of his brand of lauded violence. "If you want to throw your money around, that's your prerogative."

"Thank you," Ivan had said in that too-dark voice of his. She'd had the wild notion that he knew the way that sardonic tone moved over her skin, into her flesh. The way it had teased at her, like the lick of a dark flame. His black gaze then had mocked them both. "I do so appreciate your permission."

And that was how, barely seventy-two hours later, Miranda found herself standing half-dressed in a wildly famous Parisian haute couture house. It had all happened so fast. She told herself that was why her head was spinning—that and the time change. Or, perhaps, those old, terrifyingly familiar nightmares that had woken her in a heart-pounding, gasping panic each night since Georgetown. She stared at herself now in the range of mirrors splayed before her, clutching what she'd been assured would one day be a fantastically glamorous gown to her chest, as if that could preserve what was left of her modesty, wondering if the sleeplessness showed as much as her bare skin did.

Not that it mattered. She might as well have been a piece of the elegant furniture for all the notice anyone took of her.

Ivan was sprawled across the opulent settee that took up a good portion of the private, luxuriously appointed dressing room, all scarlets and golds, deep carpets and magnificent draperies, while couturiers and their obsequious underlings fawned all over him. They plied him with champagne and small silver trays of hors d'oeuvres, laughed uproariously at his passable French and treated Miranda exactly the same way he had since they'd arrived hours earlier: as the nameless, no doubt interchangeable mistress he was dressing for his own amusement today, her feelings on what pieces were selected to adorn her unsolicited and unimportant.

She hardly recognized her own reflection. She felt as if she was in some kind of time warp— that if she stepped outside, it could be the decadent Paris of any past century, and she the kind of fallen woman who would consent to the seedy arrangement they were pretending to have. She shook her head slightly, as if that could clear it of leftover nightmares and time-change grogginess. As if that could make this okay.

Was she really dressing for a man's pleasure, at his command? Had she really climbed in and out of outfits at a wave of his hand, marching in and out from behind the privacy screen erected in the corner at a word or two from him, trying on this or that depending on his expression? Had she really let him pick out an entire wardrobe for her this morning, as if she'd come to him naked and with nothing?

It had been one thing to imagine it in her head, this calculated fake relationship with very clear goals that had seemed almost inevitable, even reasonable, in that suite of his in Georgetown. But it was something else entirely to make herself *do* it. To let all these haughty French strangers assess her so coolly, to let them think they knew exactly how she would pay for the piles of ready-to-wear pieces Ivan had decreed acceptable for *his woman*, all of it packed away already into glossy shopping bags as he turned his attention to the crucial matter of the gowns she would wear on two red carpets and at his benefit over the next six weeks.

It's the jet lag, she told herself, again and again. *It's making you maudlin. It's making everything seem so much* more *than it really is, so much* harsher *somehow, and the nightmares certainly haven't helped.*

But what she heard was that Russian-spiced voice of his, calling her *my woman* in his offhanded way, the sound of it echoing around and around in her head until her chest felt tight.

Ivan glanced up then, and caught her gaze in the gleaming bank of mirrors. She could see that focused fire in the depths of his black eyes, and was aware, anew, of the length of her naked back that was exposed to him, the glorious, shimmering blue fabric they'd pinned onto her yawning open almost all the way down to the top of her panties, which were the only thing of hers she wore.

She might as well have been naked, suddenly. She felt naked.

Like she was no more than an object, displayed for his brooding perusal.

Which was, of course, exactly what she was today, Miranda reminded herself sharply. Exactly what she was *supposed* to be. They'd agreed. *She* had agreed.

This was too much. It was too disturbing. She couldn't do it. She couldn't *do this*—

His lips moved then, distinctly. And though he only mouthed the word, for her eyes alone, Miranda heard it like a thunderclap. As if he'd shouted it.

Public.

"We agreed we would only put on our little act when there were cameras around," she'd said nervously when they were somewhere high above the Atlantic Ocean, and Ivan had settled into the wide seat across from her with a glass of wine in his hand.

Too close, she'd thought in a rising panic. He wore a white button-down shirt, crisp and untucked, that only hinted at the impressive strength beneath. And those intriguing tattoos—the one she'd seen on his arm and the teasing hint of another she could see in the open neck of his shirt, inked black on his golden skin. He'd been sitting much too close, and he'd been much too compelling, and she'd had no time to process any of this.

She'd returned home from Washington the day after their kiss to find paparazzi camped out outside her apartment building high on Manhattan's Upper West Side. She'd holed up indoors, grateful that Columbia's commencement ceremony had been the week before and that she'd finished teaching all of her classes for the semester. She'd pretended that none of this was happening, that everything was as it had been, that she'd never met Ivan Korovin. Or kissed him. Much less made this devil's bargain with him.

And when the denial had run its course, she'd planned out her new book and calmed herself with bright and happy visions of her future. When he was out of her life. When she could analyze and shape and process all of this as she wished. When she could discuss that kiss in her own terms, on all the networks that had been clamoring to interview her.

When the nightmares faded away again, the way they had before she'd met him, and let her sleep.

She hadn't been ready for him so soon after Georgetown. She hadn't been prepared for the shock of it when he'd greeted her in the sleek silver car that had whisked them both to the airport, much less the scorching *force* of him once they'd found themselves alone in the sitting area of his private jet, his men up in the front or disappeared into the staterooms.

"We did not agree." He'd drunk from his glass with apparent unconcern. "You made an announcement. I sense you do so often."

She'd ignored that last part.

"Does that mean you don't agree, then?" she'd asked tightly, aware only when his gaze had flicked down to her hands that she'd been clenching them too hard against the armrests of her deep leather seat. She'd forced herself to let go.

"As a matter of fact, I do not." He'd met her glare with that irritatingly calm gaze of his, that had held, as ever, a simmering amusement in its brooding depths. She hadn't wanted to ask herself why that affected her so much. Why it burrowed so deeply beneath her skin. "We will put on this little act, as you call it, when we are in public. Only when we are alone, just the two of us, will we drop it."

"But—"

"Cameras are everywhere," he'd said quietly, with that edge of quiet, implacable certainty. "Eager eyes and mobile phones set to record. Gossiping mouths with instant internet access. You think you know what it means to be in the public eye because you have appeared on some television programs, because your name is known in some circles." His mouth had curved slightly. Mockingly. "You don't."

There had been something in his gaze then, something dark and almost painful that made her heart seem to beat too hard in her chest. She'd cleared her throat, more confused by her insane urge to offer him some kind of comfort than anything that had come before. She'd tried to shake it off.

"That seems extreme," she'd said. "And unnecessarily paranoid."

"Yet it is precisely how I have managed to be a major movie star, featured in the number-one summer action movie for four years running, and still considered mysterious and reclusive," he'd said without the faintest shred of arrogance or pride. Only stark, indisputable fact. "This is my game, Professor. If you want a book out of it, we will play it my way."

Public.

Miranda flushed slightly now, holding his gaze in the mirrors of the opulent Parisian dressing room, as chastened as if he'd reprimanded her out loud. She forced herself to breathe. And then, impossibly, attempt a smile.

It was anemic, she thought, studying herself in the wall of mirrors, but it was there.

Ivan only watched her for another moment, and she again got the sense that she amused him, though he neither smiled nor laughed. Then, his eyes still so dark and commanding on hers, he lifted up a single finger of one hand and wordlessly commanded her to turn around in a circle.

For his pleasure.

And Miranda loathed herself, deeply and totally. But she did it.

Because that was the deal. And she would be

damned if she was the one who would break it. Not when she had so much to gain from simply… submitting to this, to him, for a scant few weeks. Surely she could do that.

Ivan's dark eyes gleamed hot when she met them again, a kind of promise there that she refused to let herself understand, even as a deeper, purely feminine knowledge fanned the flames of it across her skin. His mouth moved into something like a smile, dangerous and edgy. It made her feel too warm, as if the fabric wrapped around her had shrunk two sizes as she stood there before him.

He held her gaze, looking like some kind of pagan god of war, so tough and hard and obviously dangerous. Capable, she thought wildly, of absolutely anything.

And then, sprawled there like that with attendants on either side, he lifted up his hand and beckoned for her to come to him. Peremptory. Commanding. With only his lazy fingers and that hard, intent look on his face.

Miranda felt it like a detonation, deep inside of her, setting off a chain of explosions throughout the rest of her body. She trembled. She wanted things she refused to name, things that made her soften and burn—things she wasn't sure she understood, and told herself she didn't want to. But she didn't look away from that midnight gaze of his in the mirror. And despite a kind of deep, ravenous craving she'd never felt before, and found wholly terrifying, she didn't move.

She couldn't. She knew, with a deep certainty she'd never felt before, that if she did, if she followed the demands of this shocking, surprising yearning that ate her up inside, she would lose herself in ways she was afraid to imagine. In ways she couldn't even foresee. Forever. And she knew better than to lose her head over a man. *She knew better.*

She had to fight to keep from jumping when he stood, abruptly, scattering his admirers as he rose. Her heart seemed to drop in her chest, then started to pound, hard and slow.

Fear, she told herself, and that was what it felt like, though she knew, somehow, it was more than that. Different. *Panic.*

"Leave us," Ivan commanded in French to the people surrounding him, and Miranda didn't miss the arched, knowing looks the couturiers and assistants shot at each other. Just as she didn't miss the soft *click* of the door they closed behind them, leaving her all alone with him.

Alone and half-naked. Supposedly his mistress. She knew what they were imagining on the other side of the door. His hands, all over her. Pulling up the length of expensive fabric she wore, exploring beneath it. His mouth, hot and hard on hers. And elsewhere. She was imagining it, too.

Miranda couldn't tear her eyes from his. She couldn't bring herself to move, not even to turn around and face him. She wasn't sure she breathed.

Ivan roamed toward her in that predatory way of his, loose and yet certain, as if he could as easily take down sets of attackers with one hand as cross the elegant, high-ceilinged room to the small dais where she stood. His battle-tested ferocity was stamped all over him, on that hard warrior's face of his, on the tough and ruthless body he'd packed into dark trousers and another expensive-looking T-shirt that licked over his muscled torso, and even the tailored jacket that trumpeted his wealth at high volume, so well did it mold itself to his titanlike shoulders.

There was no mistaking who or what he was. Ivan Korovin. Desperately rich. Shockingly fa-

mous. And in complete and utter control of this
situation, no matter how keenly Miranda might
feel she was flying apart at the seams. Or even
because of it.

Her limbs ached with the effort of keeping her
upright, even her neck seemed too weak to sup-
port her head, and it was not until she saw the
movement of her own chest in the mirror that
she realized she was breathing shallow and fast.

Like prey.

"I don't want—" she began, panicked beyond
endurance, and he was *so close*—

"Quiet."

Miranda didn't know what was worse: that he
believed he could speak to her like that, that he
had the right, or that she heard that autocratic
command and obeyed.

Instantly.

It was, she knew, representative of everything
she hated about herself.

Ivan stepped up onto the raised platform and
stood behind her, and it was too much. *Too much.*
Her eyes eased closed, as if that might protect
her, from him or from herself she wasn't sure
she could tell. There was too much noise in her
head, too much chaos, and she was aware that

she was trembling—that her heart was fluttering wildly against her ribs, and she knew, somehow, that there was no way he would miss that. *He would know*—but she couldn't do anything to help herself. She felt caged. Trapped.

And somewhere deep inside, she was very much afraid that she didn't hate that feeling as much as she knew she should. It was one more betrayal in a long line, and this game of theirs had hardly started.

How was she going to survive weeks of this? When she wasn't sure she could survive another three seconds?

"Look at me," he ordered her, his voice soft and yet no less authoritative, directly into her ear. She felt the tease of his breath, imagined she felt that clever mouth directly against her skin. Miranda shuddered, but opened her eyes, afraid of what she would see.

He loomed there behind her, not quite touching her. His dark head was bent to hers, and he was so big—*so big*—his wide shoulders and his height making her seem slight and small before him. He exuded power like a searchlight, blinding and unmistakable.

And he was breaking their agreement, and she

couldn't let that happen. For far more reasons than she was prepared to admit to herself.

"You promised," she whispered, her voice only the faintest scratch of sound, hardly audible over her own heart beat. "You can't do this kind of thing when we're alone. You can't *shift*."

She could feel the heat he generated, and there was nothing but smoke and flames in his dark gaze as it slammed into hers in the mirror. Nothing but that consuming, impossible fire that echoed in her, simmering and treacherous, no matter how she ordered it to stop.

"There are security cameras in the corners," he murmured, so that only she could hear, and then he touched her.

And Miranda told herself she was the kind of woman who kept her promises, no matter how difficult, so she let him.

Ivan traced a lazy path from her wrist to her upper arm with one hand, then back down again. He could feel the way she shook with the effort of not moving, not wrenching herself away from him, and it nearly made him smile. It nearly made him spin her around and take her mouth again, and this time, with no intention of stopping.

But this was supposed to be a seduction. It was too soon.

He traced the length of her elegant spine, and ordered the fire in him to subside. But she was wrapped in a glorious spill of fabric that made her skin look like cream, and he wanted a taste. *He wanted.*

He bent his head closer, his lips so close to the line of her neck, so close that he could inhale her delicate scent. It worked through him, making him crazy. Making that razor's edge of need sharper. Making him entertain the possibility that he, too, could be seduced.

And he could see it all in the mirror. He could see that dizzy, unfocused gleam in her dark eyes, see the way his lips hovered so close to her soft skin. *So close.* He could see the immensity of his battered champion's body, the way he stood behind and all around her, the hulking brute to all her fragile, supple femininity.

The sight of it should not have made him that much hotter. But he had never been politically correct, had he? Especially not in bed.

He made himself go slowly, carefully, as if he was as in control of this, of himself, as he should have been. He held her wrist in one hand, the other moving from the small of her back to grip her hip as if he owned her. He held her the way he'd kissed her across the world in Georgetown, as if they'd been lovers a thousand times before. As if his smallest touch was a preview to a show they both knew by heart. As if he had spent hours already today thrusting hard and deep inside of her, shattering her into millions of pieces, the way he assured himself he would. And soon.

Very soon, Professor, he promised her silently.

In another life, where they were already lovers and there were none of these games, this scene would be very different. He would simply *take*. What he wanted. What he felt was his. *Her*. He would brace her against the mirrors, or have her kneel across his lap on that settee, and he wouldn't care who might be watching them. And in that life, neither would she. She would welcome it—him—with none of her suspicious frowns or patrician pearl-clutching. She would meet his every touch, his every thrust. Ivan felt that work through him, as if it was real. As if it had happened—was happening. That hard fist of desire in his belly clenched ever tighter.

"Milaya moya," he murmured, as he had be-

fore. But this time it came out like some kind of incantation. "What if I am shifting after all?"

She jerked against him, and he could see her pulse go wild at her throat. Her gaze was black, and he had no doubt at all that she would call what she felt then any number of names, but he knew what it was. He knew what her body was begging for, even if she denied it.

And it was harder than it should have been, far harder than he'd anticipated, to keep himself from claiming her right here and right now, and to hell with any security cameras.

This is an act, he reminded himself coldly. *You are supposed to be* acting.

He raised his head, slowly and deliberately, because he did not want to move at all. He did not want to let go of her. But this was meant to be a seduction wrapped inside a masquerade, and this was only the beginning. Why was that so hard to remember?

But he knew why. And he couldn't let his suicidal *fascination* jeopardize all he and Nikolai had worked for. Not even if she was the first woman to get beneath his skin, to make him forget himself, in as long as he could remember. Something he had no intention of letting this haughty little aristocrat know. He could imagine all too well how she'd enjoy using it against him.

He let go of her wrist and plucked at the fabric draped all around her, still holding her gaze, his other hand hard and possessive on her hip, because, he assured himself, it was part of the act. And because he was only a man.

"This one is perfect, I think," he said after a moment, when he was certain he would sound nothing but calm. Casual. He pretended he didn't see the shock in her gaze, the fiery passion mixed with something like betrayal. He pretended he didn't care that she thought he'd played her, because he shouldn't. Because, in the end, he was. "I like the color."

Horrible man.

"I've hired a team of stylists to attend to you," Ivan said offhandedly when they returned to his plane, as if he was addressing the help. *Horrible, awful man.* "They can accomplish a great deal in an hour-long flight. Do not argue with anything they suggest, please. I picked them for a reason."

"This is completely unnecessary," Miranda said, in a scrupulously polite undertone that felt like glass against her tongue, so badly did she want to scream at him for that little performance in the dressing room. Scream, yell. *Something.*

But there were people around, and she'd agreed to this charade. They'd even signed a few documents on the plane ride to France, just to make sure everything was perfectly clear. And more than that, her demons were her business. He didn't get to know them, which she feared he would if she let herself scream at him. He didn't get to know *her*—no matter what darkness he'd churned up in her with his little act for the cameras, what nightmares that performance would inevitably wreak upon her. It didn't matter anyway. She was going to play this role, get close to him for her own purposes and then do exactly as she liked with what she learned.

It will be worth it, she chanted to herself. *It will.*

"I don't need stylists," she told him now, impressed with how in control she sounded, when she still felt so raw inside. When she could still feel his hands on her body, like third-degree burns. "I don't need anything except a very large glass of wine and some privacy."

"I told you I have exacting standards," he said, not even glancing up from his cell phone as they climbed from the car.

And then he did, and she wished he hadn't, as that too-knowing gaze of his pinned her where she stood on the tarmac, hot and black and wildly consuming. She froze. She could hardly do anything else. His hand was warm and tough where he held her elbow so lightly, so gently, and she hated that she could *feel* it like an electric shock, sizzling through her. Just like in the dressing room, panic and reaction warred inside of her, and it took all she had to tamp it all back down.

"My game." His gaze burned into her. Merciless and hot. "My rules."

And she'd agreed, hadn't she? No one had made her do this. No one had forced her into any of it. She'd chosen to get in his car in Georgetown. She'd walked into his hotel suite all on her own. She'd agreed to this plan, she'd signed her name.

She just didn't understand why a single touch from him and she lit up inside, melting and clenching, as if he'd done much more than caress her so lightly in that dressing room. As if she'd wanted him to.

As if she was the kind of woman who *wanted*.

"Do you want the relationship we agreed upon?" she asked in a pointed undertone, pulling her arm out of his grip, entirely too aware that he lazily permitted it. "Or do you simply want to see me surrender to you in every possible way?"

His mouth curved, hard and fierce, searing into her, connecting hard to her core. Her belly. The swell of her breasts. Then deepened, as if he could see all the ways she wanted him despite herself, as if he knew exactly what she'd felt, what she still felt. What she so desperately did not want to feel at all.

But the fear of what she wanted, the fear of what she felt, the fear that these were all baby steps toward losing control and the horror she knew followed that kind of folly—that was hers. Yet somehow it made the fire inside of her burn all the brighter, as if to taunt her. She blamed him for that, too.

"Ah, Professor." It was the closest to laughter she'd ever seen him come, and something about it terrified her, as if that was a cliff she didn't dare fall over. As if that really would be the end of her, once and for all. "You say that as if I must choose."

CHAPTER FIVE

THE team of stylists presented his angry, posh professor to him with a flourish when his plane landed in Nice an hour or so later.

Ivan swept a critical gaze over her as they brought her out to him on the sun-drenched tarmac, expecting the jolt of desire that seared through him at the sight of her, but surprised by its intensity all the same. It was getting worse, he thought grimly. He'd come far too close to losing it in that dressing room in Paris, and some part of him regretted that he hadn't. It was the way she'd looked at him. It was the elegant scent of her, the heavy red flame of her hair. The impossible softness of her patrician skin. Her delicious little shivers—

It was madness. *She* was madness. He needed to stick to his plan. This was supposed to destroy her, not him.

They'd dressed her all in white, as he'd requested, the better to appear fresh and lovely next to all of his brute strength that she'd spent so much time criticizing these past years. Soft white trousers clung to her long legs, then flared gently over skyscraper wedged sandals and her brightly painted toes, which he found far more erotic than he should. They'd layered white and cream strappy tops, one over the next, to lick over her small, perfect breasts and flirt with her enticing hips. Her hair was the focal point, tumbling down in a dark enchantment of red, looking slightly tangled, as if someone—and how he wished it had been him—had been dragging his fingers through it while engaged in far earthier pursuits.

"Do I pass inspection?" Miranda asked in that tone of voice that he was developing a small obsession with. It was her snooty, ivory-tower attempt at being polite. Or doing her best to pretend she was being polite, more likely—to act the appropriate part. Her hands were on her hips, the way he'd like his to be. Not that he was at all sure he would stop the next time he got his hands on that lithe, lean body.

A dangerous game, indeed.

He wanted her in ways that worried him. And after that scene in Paris, he couldn't help but think that seducing her might come at a cost he wasn't prepared to pay.

But that wasn't anything new.

He didn't answer her, knowing full well it would infuriate her, and seeing from the flash of temper in her dark jade gaze that it did. He took the oversized sunglasses one of the stylists had handed him and slid them onto her face, covering up those mysterious eyes of hers, and indulging himself in the fleeting sensation of her skin against his fingers, the fine silk of her hair. Her hands slid from her hips, and her lips softened slightly, and he almost smiled then, because he knew exactly what burned in her then. He felt it, too.

"Come," he said. He reached over and took her hand in his, amused at the way she flinched and then ruthlessly controlled it in almost the same instant.

He doubted she understood what a lifetime of martial arts did, the ways it forced a man to be aware of his environment. That he knew when she breathed, when she held a breath instead; when she tensed, when she softened. And more. He let their fingers tangle and slide, enjoying the hitch in her breath and the deliberate way she forced herself to curl her hand around his. As if she would much rather dig her nails into his skin until he bled.

He was not a good man, he thought then, biting back a laugh. It was just as well he'd never had any illusions on that score. He was enjoying her bad-tempered, ill-fitting cloak of feigned submission far too much.

He led her over to the sexy little convertible sports car that waited for them, and handed her into it before climbing into the driver's seat. He signaled to Nikolai and the rest of his security detail, and then he put the car into gear and drove.

"We have to talk about what happened in Paris," she said the moment they started to move. "There can be no *shifting*, or whatever game you were playing. We already discussed this. You signed the same document—"

"We are in the open air," he interrupted her as if she was a fractious child. "Try to contain your need to lecture me until there are thick walls around us."

She looked at him as if she'd like to club him over the head but lacked only the appropriate instrument, and it nearly made him laugh again.

"You don't have to talk to me like I'm one of

your employees," she snapped when they slowed at an intersection.

"This is not how I talk to my employees," he assured her, amused. "They know better than to talk back."

When she opened her mouth to snap something else at him, he simply reached over and shut it with two fingers over her soft lips, testing himself. Torturing himself. *Shifting*, perhaps, whether she liked it or not. Whether he did.

"I can't wait to hear your litany of complaints," he said, his voice something too close to a growl. She jerked her head back, but he could still feel the press of her mouth against his flesh. The fire of it. The way his whole body hardened, ready for her, dooming them both. "But not right now. Perhaps you can sit back and take in the world-famous view. This is the Côte d'Azur and I am Ivan Korovin. Some people would sell their souls to be sitting where you are right now, and I wouldn't have to ask *them* to be still and enjoy it."

There was a searing sort of pause, and then she pulled a silk scarf from her bag. She tied it around her hair with quick, furious jerks of her delicate hands. She didn't say another word, and she didn't even have to look at him, this time, to convey her feelings. He had to bite back his smile. He should not find her very prickliness so delightful. It could only spell disaster for them both.

He guided the powerful little convertible along the Promenade des Anglais, the gorgeous stretch of road that separated the city of Nice from the Baie des Anges and the Mediterranean Sea beyond. He soaked in the views of the French hills in the soft light that made Provence so justly beloved the world over, the sparkling sea, and the intriguing woman beside him whose current deafening silence was only a reprieve—having more to do with the noise of the open air around them as he drove, he imagined, than any particular attempt to do as he'd asked.

It was just as well he was about to give her something to really be angry about, he thought with a certain fatalism as he guided them through the charming seaside village of Villefranche-sur-Mer and then swung out onto the small, decadently exclusive Cap Ferrat peninsula. The narrow lanes were deliberately overgrown, richly forested in lush green vines, sweeping gardens and a canopy of ancient trees. Red-roofed villas peeked out from behind private walls while the stunning views stretched in all directions—the craggy French coastline and the endless cobalt waters of the Mediterranean always just around this curve, through those trees.

Down at the tip of the peninsula, Ivan pulled into the graceful drive that led to the impressive and world-renowned Grand Hôtel du Cap Ferrat. The hotel, now deemed a palace and more than worthy of the term, was an elegant, all-white affair, trumpeting its eminence by commanding one of the finest seaside spots in the south of France.

His professor was so busy gazing up at the soaring, whitewashed beauty of the magnificent hotel before them that she failed to notice the small pack of reporters who waited near the entrance until it was too late. He knew the moment she did as she stiffened in the seat beside him.

"What are they doing here?" she asked as she pulled the scarf from her head and let that exquisite hair of hers fall free.

"I called them."

There was a small, shocked pause.

"Why would you do something like that?" She sounded genuinely baffled instead of angry. That would come, Ivan thought. It was inevitable. "This isn't one of the events that we agreed on."

He reached over and rested his hand high on her thigh, a casual possession, the way he would have if he really had been sleeping with this woman. He enjoyed the way her whole body jolted at the sudden contact. He enjoyed the way his did, too. She sucked in her breath with a sharp hiss.

"Smile," Ivan ordered her quietly as he slowed the car to a crawl. "Let me do the talking. All you need to remember is that ours is a passionate affair." He threw her a swift glance. "You want me so badly it overcame every last one of your well-documented, widely televised objections. You can hardly bear it if I am not touching you. That's the story they're here to see."

He couldn't see her eyes behind the dark glasses she wore, but he saw that fascinating color rise to stain her cheeks and the way she pulled her lower lip between her teeth. He could tell she was holding her breath and he could feel her leg quiver, ever so slightly, more a thrill than a shiver, beneath his hand. He'd already told her what those signs meant.

He'd like to tell her what he thought about how incredibly responsive she was to him, to his slightest touch or glance, and how that would work between them in the bed he had every intention of having her in, sooner rather than later. Not that he required a bed. A wall would do. A floor. This car, had they been somewhere less public. But this, sadly, was not the time.

This was work. This was his revenge. This was precisely how he could exact payment for the years of personal slights and lost opportunities. And worse, the things she made him wonder in the dark. What did it say about him that he could ignore the end and concentrate on the means? That he was enjoying it?

But then, he knew the answer to that, too.

She blew out a shaky sort of breath, as if trying to calm herself, and then she turned toward him and showed him her teeth.

He didn't mistake it for a smile.

"I dislike you," she said softly. So very softly that it would have sounded like sweet, whispered love words to anyone standing nearby. She deepened that curve of her mouth. "Intensely."

"Good," he said in the same tone as he threw the car into Park, putting his mouth near her ear and drinking in another one of her delicate near-shivers. He could start to crave them, he thought then, and he knew exactly how dangerous that was. "That always looks better on film."

And then they were surrounded.

Questions flew through the quiet air. Ribald commentary in several languages that Ivan chose to ignore for the sake of everyone's health, to the tune of all of those cameras flashing and filming, capturing every moment, every touch, every breath. He helped Miranda from her side of the car like the gentleman he wasn't and kept her close, throwing his arm over her shoulders with casual ease. He felt her tense, but she smiled as he'd commanded and nestled against his side, and for the briefest moment the press of her body against his made him almost forget himself again—made him almost forget that he was acting and she was the kind of woman who had looked down her nose at him from the start. That this was another job, a carefully calculated performance. Nothing more.

Idiot. The derisive voice in his head sounded suspiciously like his brother's.

Ivan ignored it. He fielded the questions, one after the next, with the ease of all these years he'd spent handling press junkets and intrusive paparazzi. How long had this affair been going on? Who had made the first move? What had made them act out their forbidden love in such a dramatic display in Georgetown? Was this a publicity stunt? Could they look this way, please? Smile? Kiss again?

"Surely the entire world has seen quite enough of us kissing," Miranda said, defying his order to keep quiet, but with a dry humor that Ivan knew would come across as delightfully self-deprecating. He pulled her closer, then gazed down at her as if he was filled with affection. And loved the tremor he felt snake through her, that immediate, helpless response of hers he was rapidly finding addictive. He wasn't even sure she knew what signals she was sending him, which made it that much better. Seducing her would be easier than he'd anticipated.

He told himself what snaked through him then was as simple as anticipation.

"That's it," he said when he saw Nikolai appear in the entrance to the hotel behind the pack of reporters and nod curtly, indicating the agreed-upon five minutes were up. "We'll see you all at the movies later this week."

"What about all the nasty things she's said about you over the years, Ivan?" one of the more dogged reporters asked, pitching her voice above the rest. "Have you hashed all of that out behind closed doors?"

It was an American reporter, and Ivan recognized her. Give this woman the right sound bite, he knew, and it would dominate the entertainment news. He slid his sunglasses from his face. He looked at Miranda for a long moment, until she flushed again—unaware, he was sure, that it looked as if what had passed between them in that glance was purely sexual. Carnal and burning hot. Then he looked back at the camera.

He knew exactly what he was doing. He did it all the time. It was Jonas Dark at his finest. Enigmatic. Dangerous. And impossibly, explosively sexy.

Ivan smiled. Slowly and knowingly. He dragged it out, knowing his famous smile was the most lethal weapon in this particular arsenal.

"That was just foreplay," he said.

Miranda hardly saw the cool, achingly lovely lobby of the Grand Hotel, all in elegant whites and frothy creams, with only the faintest hints of blue to beckon in the sea beyond. All she saw was that powerhouse smile of Ivan's, that he'd turned on so easily for the cameras, so sexy and treacherous. She barely registered the beautifully maintained grounds soaking in the abundant sunshine or the water arrayed before them as if the whole of the glorious Mediterranean Sea had been placed there for the pleasure of the hotel's guests alone.

She only heard him say that terrible word, over and over again. *Foreplay.* She managed, somehow, to remain silent and smiling as staff and security buzzed around them, ushering them into the sumptuous private villa set apart from the rest that she assumed only a star of Ivan's magnitude could command.

She had to bite her tongue to stay quiet. More than once.

And then, finally, they were alone in one of the private villa's luxuriously appointed rooms, filled with light and graceful arrangements of flowers. The room was done in fine yellows and clear blues, sophisticated creams and the barest hint of lavender, the fresh, crisp, timeless elegance of Provence in every detail.

And more importantly, there were no cameras. No eyes, no reporters, no snide questions polluting the air. No people nearby to hear a single word. *At last.*

Ivan moved to close the door behind the last of the hotel staff, who had all but performed grand jetés in their rush to serve his every need, and Miranda kept her word and waited until it was shut tight. Until they were finally, *finally* locked away in private.

"Foreplay?" Her throat felt clogged. Rough and cracked. As if she'd already screamed at him the way she wanted to do, over and over again. She stood in the middle of the room, her hands in fists at her sides, and wondered that she wasn't screaming now. He turned back to face her, lounging back against the door with his powerful arms crossed, his hard face impassive. *"Foreplay?"*

"Are you unfamiliar with the term, Dr. Sweet?" His voice was like silk, curling around her, sensual and beguiling, and she hated that, too. His dark eyes mocked her, as ever. "Do you require a demonstration?"

"I would sooner—"

"Careful," he warned her. Was that amusement she saw move across his fierce face then? Did he find this funny? But, of course, that was why she was so furious. She knew perfectly well that he did. "It is easy to make rash, sweeping statements in emotional moments, only to regret them later. When you are inevitably proved a liar."

Miranda was shaking again, but this time, she wasn't afraid of falling apart. This time she was far more worried that she might pick something up and throw it at his head, an urge she understood was deeply, deeply foolish. And counterproductive. But there it was, growing stronger by the second. She clenched her hands even tighter—and did not let herself reach for the nearest assortment of fat, lushly perfumed orchids in their heavy glass vase.

"Is that what this is about?" she asked, fighting to keep her voice even, though there was no pretending she was anything like calm or cool any longer. "Sex? Am I some trophy to you?"

"That would require that being with you is some kind of reward," he returned, all silken mockery and that razor's edge beneath.

There was no reason at all for that to sting. Miranda told herself it didn't—it was just this long, strange day and not nearly enough sleep. Everything stung, there had been far too much touching, and she still hadn't forgiven herself for the things she'd let him do in that dressing room in Paris. The things she'd felt. And wanted. All of which had been bad enough *before* he'd called her entire hard-won career *foreplay.*

"I deserve an award myself," she told him, battling to keep from raising her voice—sure that he would take too much pleasure in it if she did, as if it was evidence against her. "I'm no actor, and yet I'm parading around in clothes that aren't mine, with pounds of makeup on my face, pretending to think it's sexy and thrilling while you trash my entire career with one throwaway sentence—"

"Did that bother you, Professor?" he asked, his gaze suddenly harsh and intense. He pushed away from the door and moved toward her, rangy and muscled, smooth and liquid. He was mesmerizing. And a very clear threat. She knew that, she felt it in every cell, in the wild heat that enveloped her and set her heart to its panicked beating once again—but she didn't move. "Did you find it upsetting to have your life's work dismissed so easily? Made into a vicious little punch line for the masses to devour?"

She didn't like the shimmering ribbon of shame that unspooled inside of her then, making her feel too hot with it. Too low. She couldn't handle how close he was now, but she refused to let herself back away, despite every shrieking alarm inside of her that urged her to fling herself in the opposite direction. To run, screaming, while she still could. He still wore that shirt that showed far too much of his skin, that swirling hint of the tattoo on his chest, and he didn't stop moving until he was so close she had to tilt her head back slightly to meet his intent black gaze, despite the high sandals she wore.

"So this really is about revenge for you," she said, pretending he wasn't looming over her, pretending even more that her heart wasn't drumming frantically against the walls of her chest—pretending it was as simple as fear, as intimidation, when she knew very well it was a complicated mess of both. And more.

"Call it whatever you like," he said in that intense, demanding way. "Was it revenge the first time you called me all of those names in that book of yours? Caveman Number One? The Nouveau Neanderthal? When you took it upon yourself to imagine—on camera—the most insulting reasons possible for any woman I might have dated to leave me?"

"You admit it, then." Miranda pretended she didn't feel the slap of his words, the unfortunate truth of them. She remembered that sense she'd gotten in Georgetown, that he'd planned all of this, that he'd known she would walk right into his trap. And she had. "This is nothing more than an elaborate exercise in petty, adolescent revenge."

Why had she picked him all those years ago when she was working on her dissertation? There had been no shortage of widely adored, badly behaved sports heroes cluttering up the cultural consciousness, any one of whom could have made her point. Why had she zeroed in on this one?

But she knew why. She had turned a page in a magazine one afternoon and there he was, gleaming and intimidating and nearly naked, all of those muscles rippling and overwhelming, and she'd felt the punch of it. Of him. All of that rampant maleness, none of it in the least bit controlled... And she'd hated him for that feeling, for the things she felt curling inside of her, hot and wild and messy. Maybe she still did.

She sniffed now, shoving that sense of shame aside, her second thoughts so long after the fact, the probability that this was a trap she'd agreed to let him close on her. "And all because your feelings are hurt that I suggested one of your starlet girlfriends left you because you suffered from testosterone poisoning?"

"What's a little foreplay next to that?" he asked silkily, though there was a flash in those dark eyes that made her think he was choosing his words far more carefully than it seemed. "You should try it."

She rolled her eyes at him as if he didn't get to her at all. As if she was as unimpressed with and unmoved by him as she wished she was.

"How depressingly predictable," she said, temper in her voice, though she wasn't sure if she was angry at herself or at him. Or both of them. "Is there a man alive who doesn't think his magical penis can somehow cure a woman's dislike of him? It would be funny if it wasn't so sad."

"Enough of your wild generalizations and crackpot theories, Professor," he said, not in the least cowed or shamed by her words. If anything, his black gaze seemed hotter, and he was closer to a smile than she'd ever seen him get. In private, anyway, and she was annoyed that she even noticed the distinction. "Let's talk about you. And how obsessed you've been with me for all these years." He opened his arms wide, the kind of arrogant display only an excessively confident man could manage with such decidedly masculine grace, and it should have been ridiculous. "With this."

It should have been ridiculous. But instead, Miranda's head seemed to go entirely blank. His chest was hard and chiseled and acres wide. This close to him, she could sense that roaring heat and power that was so uniquely his and worse, that terrifying, betraying lassitude inside of her in response that threatened to make her simply sag against him. Simply…lie down on the vast bed she'd somehow failed to notice she was standing beside and pray he came with her. On top of her. Into her.

What is the matter with you? She didn't know how to want these things. She never had before. It was as if he'd cast some spell on her that made her someone else entirely.

"I don't want you," she bit out, desperation making her voice harsh. "Any of you."

She blinked at him, the great expanse of him. All of those smooth, hard muscles, all of which, she was far too aware, he knew exactly how to use. She'd seen his fights on television. She'd seen his movies. She wished she didn't notice that he smelled fresh and clean, of soap and warm male.

She wished she was as unmoved as she should have been.

"I want what we agreed to, and nothing more." She nodded at his chest. "Certainly not any of that."

It shouldn't have been so hard to say, and he laughed then, dropping his arms but not backing up an inch.

"Keep telling yourself that."

"You unbelievably arrogant—" she began, furiously.

"Did I ever pretend to be anything else?" he asked, his head tilting slightly to one side, cutting her off ruthlessly. His voice was calm, dark. Well nigh imperial, which was precisely how he looked as he gazed down at her. "You claimed you studied me. That you knew me. How did you think this was going to go?"

"I thought you were serious about this," she accused, suspecting that the person she was truly furious with was herself. "Instead it's been nothing but games and absurd demands, your hands on me and your constant attempts to—"

She cut herself off, but it was too late. His dark eyes seemed to glow.

"To what?" She heard it all in his voice then. Sex. Fire. Need. It pulsed in her, too. "Why don't you say it, Miranda? You might just get what you want."

God, her name in that mouth. Had he said it before? In that way of his, rich and Russian and so seductive it hurt her not to reach out and touch him? It *hurt*, and she was getting tired of all the ways she hated herself today, all the ways she continued to betray herself, all the ways this man was turning her into someone she couldn't recognize or understand.

"Oh, good," she said, proud of the way she sounded then, so close to her usual cool, almost as if she wasn't losing herself here. "Another attempt to intimidate me."

The corner of his wicked mouth simply kicked up into that mocking, compelling curve, and her mouth went dry.

"I don't have to *attempt* anything," he pointed out with a quiet certainty that pounded in her like a drumbeat. "I only have to enter a room and you begin to tremble. I only have to put my hands on you to feel you come apart."

"That's called disgust."

"You and I both know what it's called," he contradicted her with all of that easy arrogance. He was so *sure*. She told herself it appalled her. It did. "But you can deny it to yourself if you must. It makes no difference to me. Or to reality."

Miranda was shaking again, and furious with herself, knowing that he could see it—and what he'd think it meant. *What it* does *mean*, a part of her she refused to acknowledge whispered.

"We had a very specific deal," she said, trying to find her footing again. She felt like such a fool. Had he tricked her or had she been so blinded by her greed to finally get the tools to expose him that she'd talked herself into this? And now the damage was done, and she could either disappear in shame or try, somehow, to make this worldwide humiliation work for her. *Somehow.* "Red carpets, public places. There was never any talk of calling up reporters so you could make nasty insinuations and have me stand there and just… *take it.*"

He smiled then, but it was a different kind of smile, and Miranda told herself it didn't matter that there were shadows in his eyes then, that hint of darkness that she'd seen before and didn't want to explore any further. His hand moved as if he might touch her face, but he dropped it back to his side, and she told herself she didn't feel that as a loss. *She didn't.* He was simply acting. Playing his role. Her own hand rose to her neck, as if taking the place of his, and some small light flared in his eyes then, as if he recognized what she'd done.

"Did you think I would make this easy for you?" he asked then, rough and soft all at once, that darkness still heavy in his gaze. "If you want that book, Miranda, you'll have to work for it. And I can tell you right now, you probably won't like it."

"I already don't like it," she said, but it came out a whisper, and was much too dark. As if he was getting under her skin from the inside out.

"Then you'd better prepare yourself." He was even closer suddenly, so close it felt as if he was touching her, or was it that she wanted that? With parts of herself she wasn't sure she recognized? In ways she hadn't known she could want anything? "Tomorrow we go into Cannes."

His head tilted to that dangerous angle, as if he was kissing her again. His mouth was right there, wicked and delicious, and she couldn't seem to

think of a reason why she shouldn't reach across
the space between them and taste it.

But that way lay madness, and she knew what
came after. Why couldn't she remember that?
Why was she torturing herself?

"My hands are going to be all over you," he
promised, his voice dropping low, from silk to
something like velvet, rough and lush all at once.
"And yours will be all over me. I'm going to feed
you from my fingers and you'll lick them clean.
And when we get back here, in private, you can
tell me all about the ways you hated it and how
much you dislike me, but we'll both know the
truth, won't we?"

His hand came up again, and she thought he
might push her hair back from her face or touch
her cheek, but he paused. Everything went wildly
electric—white and searing. It was too hot between them, blinding and impossible, and she
knew that if she breathed too hard, it would all
be over. He would touch her and she would explode and she had no idea what might happen
after that.

Or, worse—she did know. She knew exactly
what would happen. And she didn't have any
idea how that could be true, or why what charged

through her then was as much that age-old fear of hers as it was desire. For him. As if they were made up of the same thing.

Or why she had the strangest notion that he might be able to tell the difference.

"We're not in public now," she told him from some place inside of her she hadn't known was there, her voice the faintest whisper of sound. "There are no cameras, no people. You can't touch me." She swallowed. "You agreed."

"I know the rules."

But he didn't move.

One breath. Another. And Miranda knew they were poised on a razor's edge, no matter what he said about rules, or what she'd said about *shifting*. Or what she told herself she wanted from this twisted little game.

What she did want. *She did.*

He dropped his hand and then he stepped back, as if it was harder than it should have been, and she told herself she was relieved.

"Some day, Miranda," he said, that fire in his gaze, that dark promise in his voice, kicking up that exquisite shiver all along her body, "you will beg me to break those rules. You will beg me to make that shift."

"I would rather die," she vowed. Melodramatically, it was true.

He smiled then, and it connected hard with her belly, her sex. With that great riot he'd stirred up inside of her, that she didn't have the slightest idea how to handle.

"I very, very rarely lose control of myself," he said, another kind of promise, throwing kerosene on all of those fires again, making her think that soon there would be nothing left of her to burn. "It is one of the reasons I am who I am. Can you say the same?"

And that was the scariest part of all of this, Miranda thought, staring back at him in all of that breathless tension, her body yearning for him in ways that boded only ill.

Until today—until *him*—she'd thought she could. She'd prided herself on it.

CHAPTER SIX

THE next morning, Ivan ran. Hard.

Nikolai kept pace with him through all five grueling miles, and was breathing only slightly more heavily than Ivan was when they came to a stop below the Grand Hotel, near one of the rocky beaches that sloped down into the gleaming sea. It was the sort of place he'd dreamed about when he was a boy and should have been appreciating now that it was commonplace for him, and yet all Ivan could think about was one snooty woman whose carefully orchestrated downfall should have been child's play for him. He needed only to touch her, take her. He knew it. And he'd had the perfect opportunity to push that particular envelope yesterday—yet hadn't.

He had no explanation for that. But it had kept him up half the night.

Ivan didn't speak as they walked back through the hotel's extensive grounds toward the villa. Beside him, Nikolai's silence was as eloquently disapproving as ever, for all it was ferociously cold and ruthlessly contained. Ivan almost missed the half-mad, hair-trigger creature his brother had been before Ivan had abandoned him to go off and fight the whole world.

But that Nikolai was long gone, lost to his own darkness for years now, and Ivan, too, was the civilized, Americanized version of his old self. Stripped down from his fighting weight, the better to grace Hollywood screens. Expected to be urbane and amusing as well as brutal. Fluent in the language, in the tabloids, in his own contributions to the culture. But he was still the same Ivan he'd always been, underneath. Some part of him never let go of the fact he was nothing more than the son of a factory worker, no more or less than that.

He wasn't sure he recognized the man who looked at him from Nikolai's arctic-blue eyes any longer. He'd pulled his brother out of Russia eventually, as he'd promised when they were boys. He'd taken him from their uncle when he'd been able to do it. But first he'd had to leave him. And they were both still paying for that.

"Is this your version of handling this situation?" Nikolai asked in a low voice, breaking the heavy silence between them. His gaze flicked over Ivan's expression, which was when Ivan realized he was scowling.

"It is under control."

Nikolai's frigid eyes met Ivan's. Held.

"I can see how under control you are, of course," he said, not even attempting to hide the sardonic lash in his voice. "As you run across Cap Ferrat as if pursued by the devil himself. Don't trust your brother, trust your own bad eye, is that it?"

"If you are neither my brother nor the president of our foundation while we are here," Ivan growled at him, "because you insist upon acting as the bodyguard I don't need, then I beg of you, Nikolai, play your part. And spare me the Russian proverbs."

"As you wish, boss," Nikolai replied coolly. Not at all subserviently.

Ivan dismissed him, breaking into a light jog for the rest of the way back to the villa. He knew why Nikolai was here—why he'd taken on the role of bodyguard the night that kiss had gone viral, when he'd been supposed to highlight his role as president of the Korovin Foundation in the run-up to the benefit gala in Los Angeles in June. His little brother was worried about him.

As if he couldn't properly seduce and then discard one irritating woman—who wanted him, no matter what lies she might tell to the contrary.

He ran faster. He wanted to think about other things. He wanted to shower and change, and then he wanted to take his fake girlfriend out to experience a perfect, romantic, entirely feigned day in the glare of the French sunshine and as many cameras as possible.

Because he could control that. And her. And he very badly wanted to feel as in control as he normally felt. His rules trumped her Greenwich, Connecticut, pedigree, her years of fancy, expensive education. His rules meant he could touch her like she was already his. Like he'd already won. It was his game, and she didn't need to know how close he'd come to taking her two separate times yesterday. How close he was to forgetting why he was doing this at all.

All she had to do was obey.

The nightmare struck again in the night.

It was always the same. Laughter and a giddy kind of hope, the summer evening pouring in from the wide-open windows of a small car. The hum of the cicadas, the hot, humid dark all around. And a sweet, perfect kiss that went on and on and on, making her heart swell, then beat happily inside her as she walked up a stone pathway toward a pretty brick house. And then it all turned, the way it always did, into horror. Angry faces, terrible words. Shouting. Blood and pain. Her desperate, terrified screams that no one ever heard.

Miranda bolted awake with those same screams in her ears and scraping at the back of her throat. There were tears coursing down her face; her heart galloped in her chest and it took her a long, long time to settle herself again. To breathe normally. It was the middle of the night in a foreign country and she was still so much more afraid than she wanted to be, than she thought she should have been. She blamed Ivan Korovin for that—for tearing her back open. But there was nothing to do at 4:13 a.m. but curl up in her decadently comfortable bed, piled high with exquisite linens and the softest feather pillows, and wait for the terrible images to fade. For the sun to rise and save her from her own head. Her own past.

She sat on the balcony outside her bedchamber now, a pile of tabloid magazines spread out before her on the small table, the glorious Cap Ferrat morning sun bathing her in gold and clearing her head. Doing its job.

She'd kind of lost it there yesterday, if she was honest. It was all that *touching* in Paris and in front of those reporters. All those *feelings* that went along with it that she'd been so unprepared for. Of course, the nightmare had felt even worse than usual. Of course, it had struck back. She should know her old enemy better by now, she thought then.

And her new enemy, too.

She stared down at the tabloid pictures of her with Ivan, in the sleek little convertible and snuggled up next to him outside the hotel. If she didn't know otherwise, she would have thought exactly what everyone else looking at these pictures would think: that this was a scorching affair. That she had been swept away, straight off her feet, by this man, despite all of their well-documented acrimony. Fairy Tale in France! one of the headlines screamed, and it wasn't hard to guess which one they meant. Ivan was the obvious prince, widely regarded as charming by his legions of adoring fans, and that made Miranda some kind of Cinderella.

She didn't much care for the comparison. Especially because it felt so horribly apt.

She pulled the light caramel-colored sweater-wrap she wore tighter around her, luxuriating in the slide of the breathtakingly soft cashmere against her arms. Ivan might be an autocratic, demanding, shockingly arrogant man, but he certainly knew how to pick out clothes. Her own cutoff denim shorts and the easy tank top she wore beneath the wrap seemed even rattier than they really were in comparison to the confection of cashmere she'd found in one of the shopping bags from Paris.

It felt like a caress. Which in turn, made her think of Ivan, and his clever fingers against her skin. Her lips. It made her imagine what else he could do with those strong and battered fighter's hands—

"Please try not to scowl so much," Ivan said from the open doorway then, making Miranda's heart leap in her chest though she managed, somehow, to keep from jumping in her seat. "People will begin to imagine that I am not satisfying you in bed, and all of this hard work will be for nothing."

Miranda didn't look up at him. She didn't react.

She flipped through the pages in front of her and congratulated herself on her far more measured, reasonable response to him today. No wild bursts of uncontrollable flames to light her up from the inside out. No embarrassing blushes. He only took getting used to, clearly. Soon she'd hardly notice him at all.

"Good morning," she said mildly, taking a delicate sip of the coffee she'd forgotten about until this moment. She placed the china cup back down on the table very precisely, next to the French press at her elbow. "Do you consider yourself particularly narcissistic, or is it simply a natural result of your current line of work?" She smiled when she heard him sigh. "This certainty of yours that the entire world is fascinated by what you might or might not be doing in bed? It's not healthy."

She turned her head to look at him. It was a mistake.

Ivan lounged in the doorway to her bedchamber, glistening from a recent shower, wearing nothing more than a towel low on his hips, all of that perfectly molded male flesh just…there.

Right there.

That tattoo of his in all its black-inked, intricate glory, coiled down one side of his perfect chest like some kind of warning. It was a massive, somehow elegant serpent, sleek and deadly, and it swept down the side of his torso and then around to his back, as if it was wrapped around him like a kind of totem, ready to strike. There was the tattoo she'd seen beneath his T-shirt in Georgetown, encircling his bicep in some mysterious design of brambles and swirls then twisting down the length of his arm. And still another one, of three Cyrillic letters directly over his heart. It looked like MNP.

It was as if she'd fallen down hard and knocked the air right out of her lungs. Miranda's pulse felt loud and hard, so fierce she could feel it behind her eyes. In her teeth. And lower, deeper, like a kettle drum, shaking her apart.

He only smiled that smile she now knew he used when they were being watched, all sex and promise. The fact that it was fake did not detract from its potency in any way, the way Miranda thought it should. The way she wished it would, in some despair.

"You were saying?" he asked, a rich vein of satisfaction in his voice. He moved toward her then, and stopped beside her chair, reaching out to run his fingers through her hair. It was a lover's caress. It seemed almost natural, and she had the strangest urge to lean into his hand—but then she remembered where they were.

And who she was.

"What are you doing?"

It was terrible. She could hardly speak. She felt as if she'd been doused in kerosene and his strong hand against her scalp, playing with her hair, was a lit match.

"Paparazzi like to take boats out into the water, pretend to be fishermen or tourists and use their telephoto lenses to take pictures of private balconies just like this one," he said matter-of-factly. "You can say whatever insulting thing you like, but try not to show it on your face, please."

His voice was a low, insinuating murmur, and she couldn't seem to handle all of that naked, damp male skin, all of those sleek muscles, his fascinating tattoos, the whole of him like perfect, hammered steel.

"Oh," she said. Idiotically.

He let his hand drop from her hair, moving to take the seat opposite hers at the small table. It was not an improvement. He thrust his strong legs out in front of him, and she had to fight to keep from moving her chair back. He was sure to read it as some kind of capitulation. A silent surrender. And with him lounging there across from her, she had no choice but to stare at his acres upon acres of pectoral muscles, his fiercely chiseled abdomen. That lethally coiled serpent, somehow beautiful despite its deadliness, announcing exactly who and what he was, and what he could do.

It was not unlike staring into a blazing light. Complete with little black spots swimming before her eyes.

"I assume you do this deliberately," she said, forcing herself to speak past the dazed, silly feeling that made her head spin so fast. She was impatient with herself, with this absurd, outsized reaction to him. Why was one weakness or another always her first response when challenged? She'd frozen in Georgetown. She'd simply stood there and waited to be rescued, which appalled her on some deep, primal level. Why couldn't she be as strong as she thought she was when it counted?

"What am I doing?" he asked. He picked up one of the tabloids and looked at it, his expression unreadable as he studied the article in front of him. "I am almost afraid to ask."

"This," Miranda said, waving a hand at all of his bared skin. "You go out of your way to accent your physicality. It's psychological warfare at its finest. I assume that's your goal."

He lowered the paper and eyed her from across the table.

"Are we at war, Miranda?" he asked mildly, but she wasn't fooled by that tone, or the way he rolled her name around in his mouth, as if it was something sugary.

"I was under the impression that you view everything as a war." She didn't know where the seriousness in her voice came from, or why she'd shifted into it so abruptly. She suspected it was all of that naked flesh. It made her...cranky. The sun fell all over him like a caress, making him gleam golden. He looked, again, like some kind of god. Pagan and merciless, and she shouldn't find that so intriguing. So impossibly tempting. "And if this is a war, that means I'm the enemy, and you can treat me however you please, doesn't it?"

His dark eyes met hers and held. Miranda was aware of the gleaming sea in the distance, the faint, sweet breeze, the deep green of the trees. The smell of flowers and fresh-cut grass, and the sun falling over the balcony, bathing them in that perfect blue and gold French light.

"Is this a complaint?" he asked after a long moment. He jerked his chin at the papers in front of him, but he didn't drop her gaze. "Because you are not a prisoner, last I checked, and these pictures indicate that all of this is having the desired effect."

"I never said I was a prisoner."

He shrugged in that way of his, so unconcerned. The more lethal than charming prince of all he surveyed.

"You will know when you become my enemy, Miranda. Your life in tatters all around you will be your first clue."

"My life is already in tatters around me," she pointed out, not bothering to keep the bite from her voice. "I just happen to be going along with it for my own purposes. And you haven't held up your end of the bargain yet." She tapped her finger against the nearest tabloid. "I notice that there are a lot of pictures out there, salaciously ruining my reputation, kicking up the scandal you wanted. And meanwhile, you have yet to tell me a single thing about yourself."

She could see the storm brewing there, behind those impossibly dark eyes of his, though his expression remained calm—and would photograph, no doubt, as if he was gazing at her in some or other sensual form of rapture.

"If you want to know something, ask it," he said lightly, though she could hear the steel blade beneath a seemingly mild tone like that. She could see it in that warrior's face of his. "If you are waiting for me to spontaneously volunteer something, it will be a very long wait."

"Why are you giving up Hollywood for philanthropy?" she asked.

He shifted in his chair, and rubbed those letters over his heart with one hand absently.

"There are other ways to fight," he said after a moment, in an odd tone. "Perhaps better ways."

"Why did you start fighting?"

His brows arched slightly, and there was a kind of very old, very deep hardness in his gaze then.

"I was good at it."

She blew out a breath when he didn't elaborate. When she could tell that he wouldn't. "That's not an answer."

"It is the correct answer to that particular question." His voice was implacable, and there was something terrible and ruthless in his gaze. Although she wondered, suddenly, what was behind all of the harsh power he carried with such seeming ease. All of that heavy steel. Was it that darkness she saw glimpses of now and again? Or something else—something worse?

"That's not much of an answer, either."

"Perhaps you should ask better questions."

"If you can't tell your own story," she said softly, "how can I trust that you'll tell me anything at all?"

"I know what you want to hear," Ivan said, and there was no doubting that deep, inky darkness in him then, something sharp and sad and fierce in his black eyes, in his rich voice. "Was I born the vicious monster you see before you today, made of equal parts temper and violence, a perfect fighting machine? Or did I perhaps do only what I had to do out of desperation, using my fists to escape far worse? I already know what you think of me, Professor. I have no doubt that you expect a tale that perfectly matches the character you've had in your pampered head all these years." That hard mouth moved, as if he was biting back something far worse than the bitter words that fell like bullets between them on the small table. "But only one of those things is what actually happened."

"Is this how you keep your promises, Ivan?" she asked, fighting to keep her expression smooth, her posture easy against the hard chair. As if she hadn't felt every last one of those bullets. As if she didn't feel riddled with them. "I'm bending over backward to do the things you want me to do, and you can't even answer a simple question?"

"Yes, of course," he said, and there was that hard edge to his voice then. "This is a great and terrible sacrifice for you. I keep forgetting."

She hated the way he said that, as if she'd insulted him. And hated even more that she cared whether or not that was true. When had that happened? What could it mean? She was afraid she wouldn't much like the answers to either of those questions, and so she shoved them aside.

But she couldn't pretend he hadn't pushed her off balance again, without even seeming to try. Dizzy, confused—she was sick of feeling this way. She wanted to believe it was just the jet lag. The relentlessness of her recurring nightmares that she knew were because of him. She told herself it was.

"Of course it's a sacrifice," she choked out heedlessly. Foolishly. He only looked at her in that dark, cold way, and she felt it inside of her like a blow. And hated that, too. "I don't like to be touched."

Miranda could not believe she'd said that. Not out loud. If she could have snatched the words back from the air between them, she would have.

Ivan stared at her as if she was an insect.

"By the likes of me," Ivan said, his voice a kind of harsh, terrible growl, and that hurt even more. "Rough and uneducated brute that I am. I understand. It is a tremendous sacrifice indeed. You might as well fling yourself on the nearest bonfire for relief, such is the extent of your suffering at my hands."

"I don't mean that," she blurted, flustered, something about that awful look on his face twisting through her, making her ache in new and strange ways, making her doubt herself and hate herself all the more, and she wasn't even sure why. Or why she couldn't seem to stand the thought of this man in pain. "I mean—at all. In general. Not just by you."

* * *

She could not possibly be saying what Ivan thought she was saying.

It was impossible. He knew it was impossible—he'd been the one touching her in Paris, for God's sake. He'd kissed her in Georgetown. He'd watched her fight it, yes, but then lean into it, soak it up. He'd drunk in all her exquisite responses, the shivers she couldn't hide and the tremors she fought to repress, the glaze in her eyes, the softening of her body when she'd stood tucked up beneath his arm. And he forgot, then, that all of that had been supposedly calculated on his part. He just knew it was real on hers.

"Exactly what are you saying?" he asked, searching her face for clues.

He saw only that delicious heat, climbing up her cheeks, and the sheen of acute embarrassment in her dark jade gaze, making them seem blacker, deeper. She swallowed, and then pressed her lips together, firmly, as if fighting to calm herself.

"What I just said." She shrugged, a defensiveness to the movement that he imagined she had no idea betrayed her as much as it did. Why he found it fascinating was something else entirely. "I believe in mind over body. That's what matters to me. My mind. Everything I've done to get to where I am is because of it." She looked at him as if she expected an argument, and when he only regarded her in silence she sat up straighter, taller. Gathering herself. "I graduated from high school at sixteen. I entered my Ph.D. program before I was twenty. I was always focused on work. Touching is…" The flush on her cheeks deepened. Her eyes looked almost glazed. *Panicked*, Ivan thought. "Has always been completely incidental to my life in every way."

"So you are frigid."

He knew, categorically, she was no such thing. But did she know it? Was it possible she didn't? Or was this some kind of twisted mind game women like her played with men like him?

"Of course not." Her eyes cleared slightly, then narrowed as she looked at him. As if she was offended by the question.

"Are you a virgin, then?" He couldn't help the way his mouth curved at the idea, as if he was the very caveman she'd accused him of being. He shouldn't have cared. He shouldn't have wondered, suddenly and with far too many detailed images, what it would be like to be her first. "Chaste and untouched?"

"Yes," she replied, her voice tart. Offended, perhaps. Or simply annoyed. "And I am also a unicorn. Surprise!"

"Then tell me what you mean," he said, ignoring the sarcasm. Almost enjoying it, if he was honest. "Because the mind and the body are not separate entities, Miranda. Surely they taught this in one of your Ivy League schools. You cannot choose between them. They are one and the same."

"I'm sure that you think so." She did that dismissive thing with her hand again, waving it at him as if to encompass everything he was. He wanted to catch it with his. Bite it. Put it to far better use. "You would."

"Tell me," he said then, as mildly as he could, which was perhaps not so mildly after all, "how do you suppose I became the greatest fighter in my generation? Because that is what I am. How do you imagine I forced myself to train when I was no more than a collection of agonies and bruises, and there was nothing ahead of me but more of the same?"

"Masochism?"

Ivan eyed her for a moment. Training had not brought out the masochist in him, but she might.

"My mind." He almost smiled at her expression. "Yes, Professor. I have one."

"If you say so," she replied, sweet and acid all at once.

"So tell me about these lovers of yours instead," he said then, lounging back in his chair. He didn't know why he cared what lies this woman told herself. How could it possibly affect what would happen between them—what he would make happen? And yet here he was asking anyway. "The ones for whom touch was as unimportant as it is for you."

"Some men are motivated by intellect," she said loftily, clearly insinuating that he was not one among them. Reminding them both of his place—but he couldn't tell if it was a deliberate slight or not. He let it go. "And there are more important things than sex."

He only looked at her, brows high.

"I never said I didn't have sex," she said, scowling at him. "Only that it wasn't the central focus of the relationships I've had."

"I understand," he said, almost amused then. He felt very nearly benevolent, while anticipation nearly crippled him with its intensity. "None of them satisfied you. No wonder you think such things."

She sighed. "Because you, of course, believe that you deeply satisfy every woman who's ever crossed your path, is that right?" She rolled her eyes. "What a shock."

Ivan discovered, to his great surprise, that he was enjoying himself.

"My woman," he said, very distinctly, "is, by definition and my personal preference, satisfied."

Miranda looked unimpressed. "I think you should consider the possibility they were all faking to preserve your obviously gigantic ego."

"Shall I prove it to you?" he asked silkily. And he wanted to. He did. More than was either wise or safe.

His challenge sat there for a moment. Her dark red hair caught the light, gleaming like a simmering fire, and he wanted her the way it seemed he always did. Despite his own intellect and reason, the very things she clearly thought he lacked. Perhaps she was right—perhaps, around her, he reverted to the animal she already believed he was.

"Why would you?" she asked, and he heard that catch in her throat, betraying her all over again. "I'm not your woman."

"I could still make you come," he told her quietly, not only to see her jerk in her chair, though he could admit he enjoyed that far more than he should have. "And I will. It is inevitable."

"Back again to sex," she began, in that professorial way of hers, as if her cheeks weren't that intriguing shade of scarlet. As if she wasn't breathing too fast or moving in her chair like that, as if she ached the way he did.

As if she thought he couldn't tell.

"This is all about sex," he said, cutting off the lecture before she could start. "That's what the world wants to see. That's what we're giving them."

"That's the game." But her soft mouth trembled slightly, and there was that anxious line between her brows. "It's not real."

"You're forgetting all of this chemistry," he said. He tapped his fingers against the papers spread across the table when she frowned at him. "Do you really believe this would look as good as it does if there was no connection between us?"

"Of course it would," she whispered. As if she was trying to convince them both. Almost as if she was desperate. As well she should be, he thought, and not that it would save her either way. Not now. "You're an actor."

"Yes, Miranda," he said gently. He deliberately held her gaze with his, daring her to deny it. "But you are not."

CHAPTER SEVEN

ONE day bled into the next. The beckoning blue of the sea, the cerulean sky arched high above, the dazzling beauty everywhere she looked—and then Ivan there in the middle of it, darkly compelling and far too powerful, playing his part too easily and too well.

Whenever they left the hotel, the cameras followed and their every movement was recorded, just as he had promised would happen. That meant she had no choice but to play the adoring mistress in the middle of a blistering affair, whatever that meant.

The truth was, she had no idea what it meant. How could she? But she was quickly learning what it *looked* like.

"I'm sorry you don't like touching," he said on that first day, after that uncomfortable conversation on the balcony, as he started the car and slid it into gear. "But I'm afraid we have no choice."

"I didn't ask you to change your behavior in public," she told him, irrationally furious suddenly.

Because of that sly, mocking tone in his voice. Because she hated that he knew anything about her, especially something so personal, when she was supposed to be the one learning key details about him. Because of all of this madness and trouble, none of which would be happening if he hadn't kissed her in the first place.

Because he thought he could make her come.

"I didn't complain," she continued stiffly. "You were the one who started talking about sex—no doubt to divert attention from the fact that you refuse to answer any of my questions."

"That, yes," he agreed, laughter in his voice. "And also because I like sex. A pity you do not. We could have had such fun."

"Somehow I don't think *fun* is the word I would use to describe sex with you," she'd said drily, and then everything had tilted and rolled when he'd reached over and slid a hand onto the nape of her neck, pulling her head around to his. Controlling her.

Thrilling her.

Stop talking about sex with this man, she ordered herself with no little desperation. *You can't handle it. Or him.*

"No," he said in that way of his that seemed to cast a shadow over her, as if he could block out the sun if he chose. "It's not the word I would choose, either. But it's the only one that wouldn't scare you."

"I am not—" she began, but his scorching black eyes dropped from hers to her mouth, and it shut her up as easily as if he'd used his fingers once more. Or, worse, his lips.

When he looked up again, she was mute with anxiety and he was smiling.

"No," he said, mocking her. He slid his hand away, leaving only confused longing in its wake. "Not scared at all."

Miranda couldn't seem to catch her breath. Or find her balance.

And Ivan, it turned out, was very, very tactile. She would have said that he did it simply because he knew she didn't like it, but there was a certain wildness in his gaze when he looked at her that kept her from accusing him. That made her think he liked touching her, and not simply because he was playing a game. That made her wonder what words he would have chosen, after all.

But she didn't want to think about that.

The days became a dizzy mess of his hands at her waist, on her hips, at the small of her back. Always on her, always warming her, possessive and demanding at once, as if they were not only the lovers they pretended to be, but also as if he was very much in command of their affair. The idea made her shiver. There was that fire always burning in his dark eyes, keeping them both alight. There was his warm, strong hand around hers, helping her from the car or tugging her down the narrow bustling lane of Rue Meynadier in Cannes to look at the souvenirs and nibble on olives and cheeses and sweet *macarons* from the local emporiums.

Ivan offered her a piece of local cheese out in the busy pedestrianized street that first day, but wouldn't let her take it from his hand. As he'd promised he'd do, she remembered, while delicious heat flooded through her, making her stomach tighten.

"Open your mouth," he ordered her, not particularly nicely, that steel beneath his voice again. That command. "Pretend you're at Communion, if you must. I have no doubt there are sins aplenty you'd do well to confess."

"I am neither a child nor an invalid," she replied with that forced smile that she'd kept welded to her face since they'd left the villa. "I don't think anyone will want to see you treat me—"

"As the shy and biddable maiden you play on television?" he asked blandly, popping the cheese into her mouth. She was aware of too many things at once, then—the burst of savory flavor, her own annoyance mixed with that dangerous yearning and that sardonic gleam in his dark gaze in the crisp brightness of the French afternoon. "No, you're right. That would be too unbelievable a character change."

She glared at him. He smiled at her.

But in the glossy pages of the tabloids the next day, it looked like sex. Like giddy laughter between lovers. *Like foreplay*, it pained her to admit. Hot and wild and delicious, as if they were consumed with desire right there on the street, surrounded by so many gawking tourists. As if he'd done exactly what he'd promised he could do, and well.

She felt invaded, encroached upon. Under constant attack. How could she feel anything but? And still, when they returned to the villa and to themselves, to the reality they could only indulge in private, there was some part of her that missed his hands, his smile, that harsh masculine beauty that was so much a part of him and that she was growing used to having so close to her at all times.

It should have appalled her.

"Can I help you with something?" he asked one evening as they stood in the marble entrance of the villa.

They'd spent a long day in one of the quint-essentially European hill towns that clung to the side of a particularly steep slope far above the sparkling sea. They'd leaned into each other as they'd navigated the winding, twisting little streets that circled all around and seemed to tie themselves in knots, the stone walls echoing back their own footsteps like the insistent sound of Miranda's heart all the while, drumming away behind her ribs, too fast and too hard, and all because he was touching her like that.

"What?" she asked now, only realizing as she said it that she'd been staring at him, the foyer seeming like a vast, chilly expanse between them when she was used to him plastered up against her. When she was used to the scent of him all around her, even on her own skin. His heat, his casual strength. She swallowed nervously. What was happening to her?

"Is there something you want, Miranda?" he asked, and that tone of his licked into her, fire and velvet. Ache. Want. His eyes met hers. "You need only ask."

"No," she whispered, because her throat didn't seem to work, her skin felt stretched thin and she knew exactly what that look in his dark eyes meant. In some deep, feminine way. She knew. "I don't want anything."

Ivan only watched her for a long, searing sort of moment, leaving her in ragged pieces without saying a word.

"If you say so," he murmured when it was almost too late, when she'd almost surrendered to the heat behind her eyes or, worse, to that demanding fire deep in her belly, that only seemed to grow in intensity and scope the more time she spent with him.

"I say it because it's true," she lied, and then bolted for her bedchamber without a backward glance, not trusting herself enough to stay and prove it.

Not trusting herself at all.

Preferring the inevitability of her nightmares to all the unknowns Ivan made her think about.

One sleepy morning they strolled hand in hand along the Promenade de la Croisette that stretched the length of the Cannes coastline, packed with splendid luxury boutiques, grand five-star hotels and, at this time of year, the rich and the famous from all corners of the globe and all the paparazzi and energy that went along with them. One bright, clear evening they had drinks at the Carlton, surrounded by film stars from several countries and the people connected to them, one group more impressive and luminous than the next. Another night they ate by romantic candlelight at the world-renowned La Palme d'Or restaurant overlooking the Bay of Cannes in the art deco landmark Hôtel Martinez, Ivan feeding her bites of a crème brûlée so decadent, so intense, that she thought she might black out from the sheer pleasure of it.

Or maybe, more terrifyingly, that was him. Maybe it was the way he looked at her, that famous smile on his hard face. Maybe it was the memory of those too-confident words, that pure masculine promise, emblazoned across her like the dangerously seductive serpent that was inked into his skin.

Maybe he was much too good at his job.

He held her against him near the water in Antibes, tucking her under his chin as they stared out at the yachts and other boats dotting the azure expanse of sea before them, looking, no doubt, as if they'd been having a blissful moment instead of a whispered argument about where he'd chosen to put his hands. He kissed her temple, her forehead, as they browsed an open-air market in the old part of Nice, then he threaded their fingers together as they walked, gazing down at her as if utterly besotted.

"This is what love is supposed to look like," he told her when she rolled her eyes at one of his particularly love-struck expressions.

"In the movies, maybe," she replied. "Real love rarely comes with so many handy photo opportunities." She shook her head. "But then, you only date women who crave publicity, don't you? Maybe that's what love is in your world."

"I wouldn't know," he said with a kind of matter-of-factness that made Miranda's breath catch.

Everything froze. The whole of Nice seemed

to fade into a bright blur around him, as both of them recognized that he'd shared something with her. Of his own volition. His black eyes looked bleak.

"Wouldn't you?" she asked softly.

"There were not a lot of luxuries where I grew up," he said gruffly. "We learned to do without."

And she was too thrown by the fact he'd told her anything at all to protest when he indicated the subject was closed by pulling out his phone and calling for his driver.

They attended parties on the luxury yachts that clogged the harbors, gatherings in the splendid, glittering hotels that commanded so much attention along the sparkling coastlines, all of them filled to capacity with the gorgeous and the gleaming, all of whom knew Ivan and in front of whom he seemed to have no problem whatsoever acting the lovesick fool. The most famous Bollywood actress to the right, the newest French sex symbol to the left, and yet Ivan looked only at a professor known primarily for her well-publicized disdain of him.

And he was so good at it, she almost believed it herself.

Almost, but not quite. That would be more foolish than she could bear, the most foolish thing imaginable. It might actually kill her.

Tonight he held her in his arms on the crowded dance floor of the opulent yacht of a revered Italian director, bursting with celebrities and press from all over the globe. Miranda reminded herself that this was not a fairy tale as they glided across the floor, as he gazed down at her as if he was madly in love with her—it only needed to look like one. He wasn't particularly charming despite his smile and she wasn't under any kind of enchantment, so there was no reason to feel as if this was magical. It wasn't.

It wasn't. It was only a dance, a performance. It wasn't by choice. It wasn't real.

And still she felt his hands like brands, one at the small of her back, one holding hers tight, both searing into her. She was afraid to move—afraid to find he'd left marks on her skin. Her other hand rested uneasily on his wide, wide shoulder, and she told herself it was only logical that he should have a shoulder like that, like molded steel. That he'd fought in all of those rings across the planet to earn a shoulder like that. And it made sense that he should wear a light-colored jacket over a crisp white shirt with so much careless elegance, as if he'd tossed it on without thought and his insouciance was effortless. He looked every inch the movie star he was, sleek and beautiful in his particularly bold and undeniably physical way, turning heads even in a crowd like this one, packed full as it was of impossibly gorgeous people.

No doubt it was even reasonable that he should hold her so close that she almost brushed against him—that every step, every movement, was *this close* to pressing her breasts against the hard wall of his chest, until it was all she could think about, all she wanted, all she could imagine ever wanting—

"Are you ready for tomorrow?" Ivan asked. But there were whole other worlds in his gaze then. The heat between them, the dark night all around them, and so many speculative eyes on them. She could feel all of that, and his hands on her body, and the near miss of his chest a whisper away from hers.

For a moment she didn't know what he meant.

"The red carpet," she said finally, hoping he hadn't noticed her hesitation. Hoping even more he didn't think she'd been so distracted by him that she'd forgotten herself. Even if she had.

"Are you ready?" he asked again, his dark eyes cool and distant as he scanned the crowd around them. Always in character, save that one moment in Nice. Always seeking out the cameras, as if he could sense them.

It was all too much. The music, the crowd. Ivan. The carelessly commanding way he held her to him, making her body act in ways she didn't understand or want. All of this was too much, and she couldn't seem to think her way out of it the way she wanted to do. The way she *needed* to do.

"I don't care about the red carpet," she said quietly. "You do. What I care about is finding out about you, and despite our bargain you've deliberately kept me at arm's length. Mostly."

"My parents died in a factory fire when I was seven and Nikolai was five," Ivan said abruptly, turning his head to look directly at her, his steps slowing, though he still moved to the music. And he still held her in that impossible grip of his, as if he had no intention of ever letting go. "We went to live with our uncle. He liked nothing but vodka and sambo. Nikolai eventually took up the vodka. I preferred sambo." His gaze was so hard. So pitiless. She could feel it drilling into her, through her. Hurting her. "And I quickly learned to hate

my uncle, so I got very good at it. I wanted to
make sure that one of those drunken nights, when
he thought he could beat us both into a pulp simply because we were there, he'd be wrong. And,
eventually, he was."

Miranda was afraid to move, to breathe. He
looked away for a moment, pulling her with him
as he wove in and out of the nearby couples. If
anything, he looked colder and more forbidding,
more remote, and Miranda didn't know why that
made her ache for him. As if she of all people,
his enemy, could give him solace even if he'd allowed it.

"That's why I started fighting," he said after a
long moment. He looked back at her, and made
no particular attempt to conceal the bleakness in
his gaze. "Are you happy to know this, Miranda?
Does it change me in your eyes? Make me something less than a caveman?"

"It makes you human," she replied without
thinking, and his smile then was sharper than
that look in his eyes, and as desolate.

"Exactly what you want least, I imagine," he
taunted her, and that hurt, too. It all hurt, and
she wondered where this was going—and what
would be left of her when it ended.

Worse, for one long breath and then the next, she didn't even know what he meant.

And then she did, and that was the worst part of all. That he knew exactly how invested she was in maintaining her negative opinion of him.

And that he was right.

Miranda's team of stylists descended on her the next morning, not unlike a plague of locusts, while last night's nightmare still pulsed in her and her throat was still raw from waking up crying out loud.

"It can't possibly take all day to get ready to walk a few feet across a sidewalk!" she'd protested when Ivan had announced at breakfast how soon the preparations for the Cannes red carpet would begin.

She hadn't added, *How hard could it be?* But it had curled there between them in the clear morning air out on the terrace all the same.

"Are you basing this on your extensive experience of red carpet events?" he'd asked. He'd sounded as if he was smirking, though his hard face had remained impassive, his black gaze intent on hers.

"I bow to your superior knowledge," she'd said,

trying not to sound snide. It was unsuccessful. "As ever."

And then she'd fled back into the villa, happy to get as far away from his too-incisive eyes as she could.

She was shooed into a chair in her bedchamber's spacious bath and made to sit there while her team of five buzzed all around her. Her hair was teased and shaped, her brows plucked and tweezed, her nails buffed and painted.

It would have been boring, had she not had so much Ivan in her head. *I could make you come*, he'd said. And then he'd put his hands on her, day after day. He'd held her close. He'd danced with her and made her crave him in ways she'd never craved anything before—in ways she hadn't even known were possible. And despite all her experience to the contrary, despite everything she knew to be true about herself and her body, she almost believed he could do what he'd said he could.

It felt like some kind of revolution.

She should not have talked about sex with him in any capacity. Why not invite the wolf in from the cold, while she was at it? Introducing sex into the conversation meant it would stay there, humming between them, clouding everything, making her nightmares that much more vivid, that much more terrifying. She didn't know what she'd been thinking. It was just that the kind of sex she suspected Ivan was talking about had never been much of an issue for her before, one way or another. She'd been so young when she'd escaped her father's house for the safety and sanctuary of college, and she hadn't ever really caught up with her Yale classmates, socially or emotionally.

Graduate school had been different. Miranda might have been a bit of a late bloomer, but it had seemed to matter less at Columbia. She'd eventually had what she'd always considered perfectly nice relationships with two men she met through her studies, one for about ten months, one for just over a year. She'd gotten to know each of them over very long periods of time—years, in fact. She'd become comfortable with them long before there had been any touching, or even any dating. She'd thought sex, when they'd had it, was nice. A good way to feel connected in a very specific way to a very specific person. *Very nice*, she'd thought, but certainly not worth all the commotion.

It had never once occurred to her until this moment that maybe the two men she'd had sex with simply…weren't any good at it.

That was like a second revolution, smack on top of the first, all of it fusing together somehow and turning into some sort of internal avalanche.

Ivan, clearly, would be good at it. He fairly *oozed* "good at it."

Miranda eyed herself in the bathroom mirror as one of the stylists toiled away on her face, adding a bit of drama to her cheekbones and extra full-ness to her lips, and hoped no one would notice how flushed she'd become.

She pulled in a ragged sort of breath, and thought of his hands on her back, his arm over her shoulders. That sheer physical *intensity* of his. He had been touching her—kissing her—before they'd ever exchanged a word. He was the inverse of everything she knew. No wonder she felt so inside out.

And every time he looked at her, some part of her *wanted* to burst into flames and burn down into ash and soot. Like he compelled her to yearn for it. For him. Which was almost more discon-certing than the fact that she melted into all of that fire anyway.

She didn't know what that meant, she thought

as she tipped her head back and let one of the women work on her eyes with pencils and eyelash clamps and a palette of shadows. But she hadn't hated all of this mandatory touching as much as she'd thought she would, no matter how many times she tried to talk herself into an appropriate state of outrage.

And he thought he could make her come. He'd said so with the same matter-of-fact confidence he'd used to tell her to listen to her messages and then get in his car in Georgetown. As if the outcome was never in any doubt.

She couldn't seem to get that out of her head.

"You'll be drop-dead gorgeous," the nearest stylist told her in an accent that hinted at New York and reminded Miranda of home in this castle-like villa so far away from anything she knew. "Just like Cinderella."

This was a business arrangement, not a fairy tale. But she couldn't say that. She had to pretend. She had to smile as if Ivan was Prince Charming and her fairy godmother all wrapped up into one devastating male package, complete with wealth and celebrity and the breathless attention of the entire world. She had to laugh and agree. She had to act as if she found Ivan as fascinating as they all obviously did.

And if she wasn't precisely *pretending* to be fascinated any longer—if that was far more encompassing and real than she wanted to admit even to herself, if it lived in her and grew with every breath and she was starting to worry it might be taking her over—

It wouldn't be the first time Miranda had to pay a steep price for something she should have known better than to want in the first place. The only good thing to come of having so badly miscalculated once before was that she certainly wouldn't be likely to do it again. She'd lost her family the last time. She wouldn't lose anything else, not if she could help it.

This time she'd be smart enough to keep her mouth shut.

When Miranda finally made it down into the villa's main reception room, she felt like a stranger to herself—and looked it. She'd hardly recognized the alien creature she'd seen in all the mirrors, though she'd *oohed* and *aahed* as necessary and declared everything *glamorous*.

All part of her job, she supposed. Her performance.

At the bottom of the stairs, a man waited with two cell phones clutched in each hand, a headset clamped to his ear and acrobatically spiked hair, his impatience visible.

"Hi," she said, feeling awkward when he didn't speak. "I'm Miranda—"

"Your goal today is to maintain total silence," he said, his attention flicking to one of his phones, his thumbs moving rapidly over the keyboard. "But without looking like you're not talking." She must have made some kind of noise because he looked up, and his expression shifted from disinterested to patronizing. "I handle Ivan's publicity. Which means you need to follow my script."

"I'm not an actress," Miranda said coolly. She forced herself to smile. "So."

"No cute comments about kissing," the man shot back as if she hadn't spoken. "The whole world knows you can talk. You haven't stopped talking in years, into every available microphone. But we're selling a love story here."

"And in this love story the great vast swell of my emotions has rendered me mute?" Miranda asked drily. "How romantic."

The man's eyes narrowed.

"Craig." Ivan's voice came from the open doorway to one of the sitting rooms, a slap of sheer, raw command. "I have it from here."

Craig stared at Miranda for a moment, and she stared back as if he was an overly entitled freshman in one of her core classes, and she didn't have any idea how long that would have gone on—but one of his phones began to shrill, and he stepped away to answer it.

Which meant there was nothing to do but look at Ivan. She took her time about it, one hand still gripping the banister, and when she finally got up her nerve he had moved even closer. Too close.

He looked even more absurdly handsome than he usually did plastered across all those Jonas Dark billboards, and about ten times as dangerous. He was in a sleek black tuxedo, which Miranda had seen him in a hundred times before, in a hundred different magazines, posters, advertisements. Yet it was different, somehow, standing here with him in this perfect villa in this particularly beautiful corner of the Côte d'Azur. Dressed as she was in an over-the-top concoction of a formal gown and her face meticulously made up to look like someone else's. Someone who belonged in this life, this moment. With this man. That had been her stylists' main objective, hadn't it?

To make a Columbia professor look like the sort of woman a major movie star like Ivan Korovin would actually be seen with.

His dark eyes swept over her now, taking his time and taking in the lush, vibrant sweep of the gown she wore. It was a strapless column of bright red, a shade she would have avoided because of her hair, but of course, no one had asked her for her opinion on the color. Or the cut, or the fit, or anything else. Ivan had chosen it, so she would wear it. That was the deal. She should find that offensive, no doubt. But this close, all she could seem to concentrate on was how magnetic he was, how impossibly compelling—she could *feel* it, heating up the air between them, making it seem to crackle.

Once again, she felt like his Parisian mistress from another time. Bought, dressed, adorned. Something deep inside of her turned over, way down there in the dark, and began to glow.

"I hope you approve," she said, and her voice was too soft. Too uncertain.

Too much like a lover's.

"Stand up straight," he told her, though his voice was more husky than stern, and then he reached over to physically inch her shoulders down from where she'd tensed them up behind her ears. She hardly even reacted to his hands on her bare shoulders now, and she congratulated herself. It was like a tiny spark, not a full-on wall of fire. *Progress.* "This is not something you toss on to go to the supermarket. This is couture. Treat the dress with respect, and it will return the favor."

She opened her mouth to say something, anything that didn't involve personal revolutions or Parisian mistresses, anything at all—but his dark eyes finally met hers with the force of a midnight collision, and she found she couldn't say a word.

"Come," he said after a moment, as if he'd taken a moment to soak her in, too. As if the intensity all around them that they were both so studiously ignoring was as loud and heavy in him as in her. "The car is waiting."

He held out his arm and she took it, and everything felt raw, then. Too much. Too formal. *Too real.* Miranda didn't understand how that was possible, when this was their most over-the-top moment yet. They were on their way to walk a red carpet. To parade down an aisle so that fans could cheer and reporters could take pictures and ask preapproved questions. So that pictures of them looking glamorous and together would be plastered across the globe, subject to any number of tabloid fantasies. What was less *real* than that?

And yet.

Something in her chest clutched tight. It was the fancy clothes, maybe. The dress and the jewelry they'd given her to wear with it, that she knew he'd chosen for her as well. Her hair was swept up into a sleek chignon to show off the dangling diamond earrings and the necklace was a masterpiece of intricate stones and stunning metals, making her seem to sparkle with elegance and style. Something about the idea of him picking them out for her to wear with this dress, to make her into this impossibly sophisticated version of herself, made her heart seem to stutter in her chest.

And more than all the rest of it, Ivan walked beside her, like every girl's dream of the perfect fantasy prince.

Like *her* dream, anyway, she could finally admit to herself—a dream she'd packed away a long, long time ago and had been afraid to pull out into the light ever since. First because it had had no place in her father's vicious, terrible home. And then, later, because it had seemed so silly and embarrassing a dream next to all of her important, serious studies. All of the intellectual things she'd wanted to do. Her theories, her books. Her dreams of a tenured professorship. She'd thought she'd had to choose. She'd chosen.

Yet if she squinted, she couldn't help but think as they swept from the villa toward the waiting limousine, this would look a great deal like the very fairy tales she'd taught herself not to believe in any longer. She was dressed like a princess, a beautiful gown and gorgeous jewels to match. The whole world already thought Ivan was some kind of prince. Was that what she'd see when she saw the pictures of this tomorrow? Was this the love story Craig the publicist was selling? Would she look carried away into some Disney movie, as if at any moment she might break into song?

Somehow, she shoved everything down deep inside of her, before she broke out into either tears or songs, or worse—both. Her job tonight, she reminded herself sternly, was to smile and gaze adoringly at Ivan. To pretend she was madly and totally in love with him. No more and no less than that.

Fairy tales weren't real. Neither was the way she had to behave tonight.

And both were only temporary, in any case. They'd agreed.

She told herself that didn't hurt at all.

CHAPTER EIGHT

"ARE you ready?" Ivan asked when it was finally time. When the long queue of cars they waited in to take their turn at the red carpet finally delivered them to the arrival point.

Miranda had the sudden, intense urge to say that no, she wasn't. To call the whole exercise off. As if it hadn't already gone too far. As if there was any hope of saving herself.

"Of course," she lied.

His black eyes gleamed with something that looked a great deal like compassion, but couldn't be. Her throat went dry.

"My first red carpet appearance made me much more nervous than my first title fight," he said then. A quiet confession. Another voluntary bit of himself, and she held on to it with a grip that should have scared her. It did. "I knew how to hit, not pose. But you won't be alone."

Miranda swallowed. "No," she agreed. "I won't."

Her reward was a smile—and not, she registered, stunned, that public one she'd grown so used to seeing over the past days.

This one was private. It was his. It was slightly crooked and not at all practiced. *It was real.* She knew it was real. She felt it kick hard inside of her, then send out echoes.

It made her want to look at nothing else, for hours. Days. Longer.

But then the car door was opening and Miranda had no choice but to be swept out along with him, into the baying crowd.

A roar went up when they saw Ivan. It was a wall of people—reporters and fans, the steady stream of celebrities and all of their handlers, everyone channeled down the red carpet gauntlet. Ivan's publicist took charge of them immediately. He directed Ivan to this reporter, then that one. He ended interviews that went too long or veered into areas he didn't like. He told them where to look, when to wave, when to amp up the smiles.

And they did exactly what they were told.

It was one more thing, Miranda thought when Ivan led her up the famous red-carpeted stairs, that looked effortlessly glamorous on television and, as she'd discovered herself while filming news segments, was a significantly harder task than it seemed.

"You survived," Ivan said, gazing down at her. He'd pulled her to one side, out of the pack.

"I'm not at all sure about that." Something about the oddness of the whole evening had her smiling up at him. Spontaneous. Unguarded. As real as his smile had been earlier.

He looked startled. Something moved through his dark gaze then that she would have called regret, if that had made any sense at all.

"Milaya," he murmured, so soft it was almost a whisper. So soft it sounded almost like an apology, but that was impossible.

And then he slid his hand around the back of her neck, pulled her just that crucial bit closer to him with that bone-melting certainty and smooth male grace that was only his, and fit his mouth to hers.

Miranda felt as if she'd fainted. Or simply burst apart into a shower of tiny pieces.

There was nothing but Ivan.

No noise, no screams. No people. No red carpet, no Cannes.

Just that mouth of his against hers once again. *Finally.*

She forgot to panic. She forgot everything. She tasted him, wanted him, lost herself completely in the drugging kick and clamor of him, and then, after ages and eras, or perhaps only minutes, he pulled away. But only a little. Only enough for her to come back to herself. His big, tough hands rested at the base of her neck, his thumbs still stroking the line of her jaw, as if he might simply move her mouth back to where he wanted it in a moment, and lose them both to that wild, magical heat all over again.

Her heart thudded hard. And then again.

Miranda understood then, with a kind of painful resignation, that the things she felt about this man were deeper and far more complicated than she wanted to admit. But that didn't change the fact of them.

And it was only then, when she processed the way he looked at her, something calculating and shrewd in that black gaze, mixed in with the fire she recognized all too well, did she understand that he'd staged it.

Of course he had.

Shame and humiliation fought for supremacy then, and both left scarring marks deep inside. She couldn't believe how pathetic she was. How

gullible. Dreams of Disney movies and a Cinderella dress didn't change the truth of her situation.
It only made her unacceptably, embarrassingly
foolish.

And that didn't change the way she felt about
him either, which only shamed her all the more.

"Why here?" she asked, and she couldn't do
anything about her voice, choked and constricted,
giving her away. Much less whatever look she
had on her face then, that made him look back
at her as if he hurt, too, but she couldn't let herself think about that. It might take her out at the
knees. "Why not out in the thick of the things
for maximum coverage?"

There was something terrible in his dark eyes
then, and that mocking curve to his beautiful
mouth. And yet she knew, somehow, that this
time, that mockery was not directed at her. She
didn't understand why that made her want to
weep.

Why all of this did.

"It would look too staged," he said, with devastating honesty, a sardonic inflection to his voice
then, aimed, she could tell, once more at himself.
His gaze was so bleak. And this was all too pain-

ful, when it shouldn't have been. "Too showy. Back here we might have imagined ourselves in a private moment. It looks real. Stolen kisses, forbidden love. Who can resist it?"

Miranda knew, then, that he felt this, too, whatever this thing was that was choking her where she stood. This…*shift*, after all. It was too big. Too hot and uncontrollable and consuming. Real enough, she understood too late, to hurt this badly, to leave such deep marks inside of her.

Lost before it began.

Had she known all along that it would be like this? Had she sensed it even on that long-ago day, when his picture in a magazine had sent her down the road that had brought her here? Had she suspected that one day he would touch her like this, kiss her like this and tie her into knots she worried she'd never get wholly untied again? Tear her whole world apart so easily?

Except this was no kind of fairy tale, despite appearances to the contrary, and all Miranda was ever going to be was a convenient frog tarted up to look like a temporary princess.

It shouldn't have hurt.

It shouldn't have mattered at all. Someday, she thought, it wouldn't.

In time she would forget that look in his eyes, that shadow across his face, this great and suffocating heaviness in her heart. When this little interlude was over. When she was free of this. Of him. Of all these things she felt without understanding why.

When she became herself again.

"I hope you didn't ruin my lipstick," she told him then, managing, somehow, to force herself back into the role she'd agreed to play. To keep that threatening heat behind her eyes from betraying them both. She even smiled again, carefree and amused. In on the joke.

Maybe she was more of an actress than they'd thought.

But then his midnight eyes met hers, so hard and so uncompromising, and there was nothing but agony there. Loss. Grief for something that never could have been.

It shouldn't have mattered.

But it did. So much more than it should have. So much more than she could bear.

"Of course I didn't," he said quietly. "I'm a professional."

And then he kissed her again, because he had to or because he wanted to, or maybe something caught somewhere far too complicated and breathless between the two, and none of that seemed to matter anyway when his hard mouth claimed hers.

Hot. Demanding. *Ivan.*

Miranda kissed him back.

She knew it wasn't real. She knew it didn't count. But he tasted like smoke and Ivan and all of that longing she'd kept bottled up inside of her all this time, without ever knowing it was there. And there were truths she didn't want to accept, especially not here. Terrible truths that worked through her like pain, like heat.

Like falling in love with the man she'd vowed to hate, when she knew he was only playing. But she couldn't let herself think about that. She had the terrible suspicion it would lead only to tears, and she was in public. This was a performance.

So she kissed him instead, with all of those things she knew she'd never say, with her scared little heart and that pounding heat in her sex that was only for him, and told herself it was the best she could do. The best she *would* do.

And it was searing and right, terrible and heart-breaking, changing her forever right there in the glare of all those cameras and the whole of the watching world, damning them both.

But Miranda most of all, she feared. And possibly for good.

The plane hung high above North America, arcing its way from New York City toward Los Angeles, and Ivan stared out the window beside him as if there was something more than clouds below and sky ahead to see.

"It seems you were right after all," Nikolai said, dropping into the wide leather seat opposite Ivan, his lethal blade of a frame seeming too primal, somehow, for the sleek executive luxury of the jet all around them.

"I am always right," Ivan replied, smirking out at the empty sky. "I am Ivan Korovin. I read today that I am one of the sexiest men alive, according to a selection of fans in the Philippines. Can you say the same?"

"A great accolade indeed," Nikolai said drily. "And no doubt a tremendous comfort to our parents, had they only lived to see it."

Ivan remembered them only vaguely, gray and brisk and humorless, and felt certain that his entire life would have seemed, to them, like nothing but foolishness and vanity. That was no doubt Nikolai's point. And tonight, Ivan agreed.

"Perhaps I underestimated you, brother," Nikolai continued when Ivan offered no retort. Was that a note of admiration in his voice? Why did that make Ivan feel so cold, suddenly? "When we left your little professor in New York, she was significantly subdued. It shouldn't be at all hard to break her now."

But Ivan worried she was already broken, and unlike Nikolai, took no pleasure in it.

He'd escorted her down the metal stairs onto the tarmac in New York, then walked her to the waiting car, not wanting to admit to himself that he didn't want to let her go. He didn't want her out of his sight, or out of his reach. He didn't know what had happened in Cannes, what had blown up between them like that on the red carpet. He didn't want to think about it. But he could still feel her mouth on his, hot and sweet. He could still see that shattered look in her eyes that had had no business being there, that made no sense at all, and yet had lanced through him just the same.

He could see the photographs of the two of

them in his head, as glossy and bright as they'd been in the papers. That first, hot kiss on the Cannes red carpet. The way she'd gazed at him, as if theirs really was a love affair too intense for words. And that aching blast of need that had nearly made him forget where they were when he'd taken her mouth that second time, because he'd had to taste her once again, or die. All of it on film, splashed across the papers and the internet. All of it available to anyone who cared to look, when it still moved in him like something highly charged, electric—and private.

None of this should have been happening.

His goals were very clear. First he would seduce her. Then he would toss her aside, brutally and publicly, tainting anything further she ever said about him as the unhinged rantings of a woman scorned. Simple. Easy. Exactly what she deserved after all these years.

Except nothing was going as planned.

He'd expected to want her, because he had a weakness for smart and haughty and unimpressed with him, apparently, wrapped up in one aristocratic, obstinate package. He'd always wanted the things he shouldn't, the things not only likely to destroy him, but also certain to do so in the most painful way possible. It was a Korovin family trait. But he'd also expected to hate her, disdain her and her Ivy League snootiness at the very least, and he didn't quite understand how that hadn't happened. Or why he'd found himself telling her things he'd never told anyone before.

Or what had sprung up and taken him over like this, making him all but unrecognizable to himself. He was not a man who formed attachments. He knew better. He'd loved his parents as any son did, despite their coldness, and they had died. He'd wanted to love his uncle, until the drinking and brutality made that impossible. He had deeply admired his first trainer, the man he'd considered his savior, until he'd tried to steal the bulk of Ivan's money after the championships had started mounting up. And he loved Nikolai, still and always, and look what he'd done to him. Look what Nikolai had become.

Damn her.

"I will see you in ten days' time," he'd told her, unnecessarily, standing in the open door of the car, holding her captive between him and it.

"Yes." But she'd been hiding from him even as she'd tilted up her chin and met his gaze, that dark jade too black, too dark.

"Miranda…"

But there'd been nothing to say, and he couldn't have said it even if there had been. How could he have? She was Miranda Sweet. His loudest critic. His enemy. They'd set all of this in motion that night in Georgetown, and there was no stopping it. There was no changing course. Not now. The benefit gala drew closer by the day, and with it, the end of all of this. His revenge and her come-uppance. As planned from the start.

"Do you really think they'll hound me?" she'd asked then, her voice too quiet. Too unsure. He'd hated it. He'd wanted her spark back, her fire. He'd wanted her to feel this wildness, this mad-ness, that lived in him now. He'd wanted her any way he could have her, no matter what it did to either one of them.

"The paparazzi?" Ivan had asked her then. He'd reached over and played with ends of her dark red hair, unable to keep himself from touching her, letting the silken strands slide through his fin-gers, letting the ways he wanted her burn through him, blaze hot, make him hard and edgy and wild with need. He hadn't wanted to leave her in New York. He hadn't wanted to leave her at all. "Yes.

It will be a feeding frenzy, I imagine. Don't leave your apartment unprepared."

They'd discussed it on the flight back from France, when she'd sat with a throw wrapped tight around her and had avoided looking at him directly. As if she'd feared corrosion, or something far worse. They'd gone over what she should expect, what she should do. What he wanted her to do. What she should and shouldn't say.

But he couldn't stand the way she'd looked at him then, standing there on the tarmac, as if this was all some kind of betrayal. As if he'd done this to her. As if she hadn't agreed to it herself.

"You could have said no, Miranda," he'd reminded her, his voice harsher than necessary. But he hadn't been able to stop himself. He'd seen the way she'd tensed. As if it had hurt. As if *he'd* hurt her. And he'd loathed himself anew.

"Could I?" she'd asked, that razor-sharp edge back in her voice then, and he'd found he preferred it, even as it cut deep. "After you pointed out it would make me a hypocrite either way? I think we both know you were well aware I would do exactly what you wanted me to do, even then."

"When was this?" he'd asked in much the same way, while the heat between them roared. "I apologize, Professor. I must have missed your momentary lapse into obedience."

Her smile then had been venomous, but he'd told himself that was better than the hurt. That terrible pain he couldn't have fixed even if he'd wanted to—even if he hadn't felt the lash of it himself.

"Goodbye, Ivan," she'd said then, and climbed into the car. "May the next ten days feel like very long years."

Ivan bit back a smile now, remembering that bite in her voice.

"I don't think she is as easily subdued as you'd like to think," he told Nikolai, and didn't try as hard as he should have to keep that reluctant admiration out of his voice.

His brother's brows lowered, as his frigid gaze moved over Ivan's face, seeing far too much. "Then you have work to do," he replied. "The benefit gala—"

"I know the plan," Ivan snapped. "It was my idea, if you recall."

"I recall it perfectly," Nikolai said, as if he was worried. For Ivan. "Do you?"

His gaze met Ivan's, bold and challenging. If he had been another man, Ivan would have taken that look as an invitation to a brawl. And the way he felt right now, he would have obliged, years of guilt or no. Instead, he looked away, back out the windows, furious with no outlet.

"That's what I thought," Nikolai said.

And Ivan had no response for him. No argument. There was only the empty sky, stretching out in all directions, and he didn't know his own mind.

He didn't know what he wanted.

Or, worse, he did.

Later, Ivan stood out on one of the many terraces outside the house he'd bought in Malibu not long after he'd signed on to play Jonas Dark. It was perched on a bluff overlooking the great expanse of the Pacific Ocean, almost entirely made up of glass walls, some of which simply slid aside to let the natural beauty in. The complacent California sun was sinking toward the gleaming, golden-tipped water through layers of stunning reds and deep oranges, Miranda was across a continent from him, and he felt emptier than he had in years.

He didn't want this. He'd never wanted this. It was weakness.

She was a weakness.

He saw her gorgeous smile, so unaffected and true, making the whole of Cannes disappear in a single flash far brighter than any of the cameras. He heard the sound of her cultured American voice, the fascinating way she put words together, the sweet sting of them. He felt her in his arms, that slight, delicious little tremor that shook through her when he touched her, her fingers laced tight with his as if keeping the kinds of promises she was afraid to acknowledge. He tasted her mouth, addictive and wild. He had a promise to keep to her, and he had every intention of doing exactly that. Again and again. And not only because it was part of his damned plan.

Ten days already felt like years, and not a one of them had passed.

I'm not done with you yet, Professor, he thought, as if she could hear him. As if it would change anything if she could.

"There's something you need to see," Nikolai said.

"I feel certain I won't like it," Ivan replied, turning to see his brother standing behind him like the ghost he'd become, almost blended into the shadows, almost as dark as they were.

"You won't."

Ivan followed Nikolai through the sprawling cliffside house to his media center, where a huge television screen dominated the whole of one wall. Nikolai pressed a few buttons on a remote control and the screen filled with Miranda, as if Ivan had conjured her into being with his thoughts alone. His terrible longing for one more thing he couldn't have.

She looked sleek and calm, standing in front of her apartment building as if she routinely held press conferences there. As if she was happy to do so, in fact. She did not appear broken or wounded in the least. She was smiling prettily at the cameras as if she'd never been more comfortable in her life.

"This is alarming," Ivan noted drily.

"Just wait."

They were throwing questions at her, some speculative, some surprisingly knowledgeable, some insane. Some simply rude.

"Don't you hate Ivan Korovin?" someone yelled at her, the braying male voice rising above the rest of the din. "Didn't you once vow that your goal in life was to take him down?"

Miranda's smile deepened. Became a mystery.

"There are so many ways to take a man down," she said, that particular smile a weapon Ivan hadn't known she carried. But he felt it all the same, like a knife to the jugular. "Aren't there?"

They loved that. They howled at her, and Ivan hardly heard what they asked. He only saw the way she looked into the cameras and knew, without a single shred of doubt, that she was looking straight at him. He could see the challenge in her dark jade gaze, through the cameras, across the vastness of this wide country. He recognized an opponent when one stepped into his ring, then stepped to him.

Her smile hinted at wickedness, played with something naughty, yet never quite crossed over that line. It was vaguely familiar, he thought. It was very nearly masterful.

It was, he realized in sudden astonishment, his.

She'd obviously learned it from him in France, and he found himself torn between a reluctant admiration and a cold, encompassing fury that she would use it against him like this. No matter that he planned to do far worse to her.

"The barbarian was at the gate," she said then, so very smoothly, undermining him that easily.

With that single word—*barbarian*—she reminded the world that she'd always thought he was a Neanderthal, and let them know that she, at least, still believed he was one. As if the whole world was in on the same joke with her. Ivan felt his teeth clench hard, and forced himself to breathe.

She shrugged, looking straight in the camera, her gaze clear. "So I let him in."

He had certain promises to keep to her, Ivan thought then, that fury pumping through him and then, as it always did, turning him fiercely calculating and endlessly, diabolically patient, just as he'd always been right before he'd won another fight.

Just as he'd been before he'd crushed whatever opponent dared challenge him into an apologetic pulp.

He'd keep his promise. He'd make her scream out his name like he was her god. Like the barbarian she believed he was already. He would take great pleasure in making her pay.

And when he destroyed her, the way he'd always planned he would, he told himself he wouldn't even care.

* * *

Miranda stepped off the plane into what was, in June, already the arid height of summer in Los Angeles. The dry heat was like a hard slap, fierce and uncompromising. The ubiquitous palm trees stretched toward the hot blue sky overhead, and the hills were toasted gold and brown, looking mellow and easy despite the temperature as they sloped into the waiting sea.

Miranda herself was determined. Resolute. France had been a disaster, she'd decided in her ten days of Ivanless solitude, and largely of her own making. She'd lost her head and then, somehow, herself. She'd let all of this become far too complicated.

It was a business deal, not a fairy tale. Fairy tales were stories for lost children, not grown women. It was time she acted like the adult she was.

"Do you think it is wise to declare war on me?" Ivan had asked her over the phone, not long after he'd left her to the paparazzi in New York City. Not long after Miranda had decided to reclaim some small part of what she'd lost. What she'd surrendered.

"You are the undefeated champion in the mixed

martial arts ring and on various movie screens," Miranda had replied coolly. "But in the court of public opinion, I think we're tied."

"That, Miranda," he'd barked, "is because I have not been fighting you. Yet."

But he couldn't help but fight, whatever he did. And she knew him now. Better than she wanted to. So well, in fact, that it had invaded her already fractured sleep. Nightly. She woke up in the small hours, breathless. Yearning. Shaking from the aftereffects of the disturbingly passionate images that chased each other through her head, too vivid and too carnal. Too infused with longing and lust. Too real.

Dreams of Ivan chased her usual nightmares in a loop. Long-ago summer evenings mixed with the sweet Cannes breeze, Cap Ferrat shattered beneath the inevitable pain and fear, Ivan himself appeared in scenes of that same old nightmare as if he'd taken that over, too, and all of it was swept through with that wild, unshakeable *need*.

None of that mattered, she told herself now, sitting quietly in the back of yet another one of Ivan's endless fleet of cars. She stared out the window as the car drove north along the famous Pacific Coast Highway, taking her much too quickly through beach communities like Venice and Santa Monica that she knew from a thousand television programs and heading straight into the legendary heart of Malibu.

It should not have surprised her that Ivan lived in a house of glass and architectural whimsy, perched on the edge of a rocky outcropping over the mesmerizing shift and roll of the ocean. It was bold and demanding, much like the man. It did not fade into its surroundings, nor did it lord itself over them. It simply was. It commanded attention and respect.

I'm in so much trouble, she thought as she was driven to the front door at the top of the sweeping private drive, surrounded on all sides by proudly jutting palm trees, sweet-smelling bushes of fragrant jasmine and great tangles of bougainvillea vines in magentas and purples, a riot of bright color and soft scent before the punch of that hard, cold house beyond.

The equivalent of that smile of his, the public one, and the formidable truth of him to back it up.

She climbed from the back of the car, reluctantly, and stood there for a moment as it pulled away again, headed for the separate building she assumed was the garage. She looked around as the breeze flowed in from the sea and the hills, cutting the heat, smelling of smoke and rosemary, the faint hint of eucalyptus. Salt and flowers.

She was in so much trouble.

She'd spent all of this time locked away in her apartment five flights above the busy Manhattan streets, desperately trying to distill her experience in France into cool, incisive, purely academic sentences. Trying to describe what it was like to spend all of that time in such close proximity to a man like Ivan in the detached vocabulary of her profession. Trying to write the damned book that would make all of this worthwhile.

And had instead found herself staring off into space, reliving every time he'd brushed his fingers over her neck, her hand, her cheek. Feeling it as if it was happening all over again, as if, were she to close her eyes, she would open them to find him there in front of her as if summoned by the force of her yearning, all of that dark promise burning in his eyes as he gazed at her.

It was pathetic. Not to mention dangerous.

And it didn't matter anymore. It couldn't. She'd been so naive—expecting that a man who'd made his life a temple to the physical wouldn't be...

incredibly, impossibly tactile. All about skin, bodies, touch. Of course he was. *Of course* he'd overwhelmed her. In retrospect, she should have known it would happen. She suspected he'd known exactly what he was doing—and she should have anticipated that, too.

But she knew now. And he couldn't have the same effect on her if she was expecting it, could he? No matter what she felt for him. No matter what.

The air changed, then, though there was no noise. No warning. Only that ineffable, inexplicable shift. Her skin prickled. There was the slightest chill down her spine, and her stomach flipped, then knotted.

And when she turned her head, he was there.

CHAPTER NINE

IVAN stood in the open doorway, seeming to fill it. His arms were crossed over his mouthwateringly bare chest, his tattoos sinuous and seductive over all of that hard male flesh, his black eyes trained on her just the way she'd seen them in all of those hot, naked dreams that still moved in her, making her head spin. Or perhaps that was the ordinary, inevitable effect of Ivan standing only a few feet away wearing nothing but a pair of loose black trousers low on his hips, leaving even his feet bare.

Miranda's mind went blank. Her body exploded into a host of reactions she would have thought meant the onset of an intense and sudden illness had she not known better. Had she not understood by now that it was him. It was all Ivan. This desert in her throat, this flood of scalding heat between her legs. This breathless whirl of sensation, this spinning wilderness in her head.

Ivan.

Their gazes clashed. Burned.

Miranda thought there should have been a storm—sudden thunder, torrents of hail, the sizzle and pop of summer lightning—but the California sky was a calm and sleepy blue all around them.

It was Ivan. He was the storm, and Miranda was terribly afraid he was already inside of her, changing her, uprooting her and destroying her, without his having to do anything more than *look* at her like that.

His hard mouth curved, though she didn't make the mistake of thinking he was truly amused. Or even really smiling, come to that.

He lifted one of his hands and crooked his finger at her in the universal signal to come, just as he had once before in a Parisian dressing room.

Like he was some kind of Russian prince after all, beckoning the peasants near, wearing so little, wanting only her instant obedience in return.

Expecting it.

"Do you think I'll come running?" she asked, not moving. Hardly daring to breathe. Afraid her feet would betray her of their own volition.

That curve of his mouth hardened, made her chest feel tight. "Feel free to crawl."

Miranda reminded herself that she was brave. That she was strong. That he was, as he'd once told her himself, only a man. Not a monster, despite what she'd long wanted to believe about him. Not capable of *making war* on her unless she let him. He was only as in control of this—of her—as she allowed.

"I've had a long flight," she said. She smoothed her hands down the front of her floor-length black sundress, hoping it hid her nerves but suspecting from the way he tracked the movement that it did the opposite. She pushed on anyway. "I want something to drink. Maybe a nap. I don't have the energy for this."

"'This?'" he echoed, and now he did sound amused.

"You."

Ivan's dark eyes narrowed slightly. He didn't move. He simply stood there like the warrior he was, and he was, she thought, the most intimidating man she'd ever seen. The most formidable. And he terrified her, but not, she'd come to understand over the past ten days, in any of the familiar ways.

Miranda made herself walk toward him. She told herself there was no need to be the least bit intimidated, and still, that thunder rolled inside of her, that lightning crackled deep beneath her skin. That storm raged inside of her, mocking the perfection of the day.

You can do this! she congratulated herself. *You can't control him, but you can control yourself—*

Ivan reached out again when she drew up next to him, and caught her by the elbow.

"Miranda."

That was all. Just the lightest of touches, a brush of his hand. Her name.

But that was all it took.

The world sizzled, burned to white, then simmered red. Like everything simply burst into flame, incinerating her. Leaving her nothing but red-hot embers and that driving, incapacitating need.

For him. For *more*.

She didn't know who moved first. Who closed the distance between them. But his mouth was on hers, hard and hot. Her hands were buried in his thick dark hair as she kissed him back, greedy and wild. There were no cameras here. No one to watch them, record them. Report back.

So there were no brakes. No boundaries. Nothing to stop the impossible rush of pure sensation.

Miranda stopped fighting and wrapped herself around that hard, tough body of his. That warrior's physique, so roughly hewn and finely muscled. Finally, her breasts crushed into the great wall of his chest. Finally, she explored that breathtaking sweep of hot, chiseled male beauty that was his back, his waist, with her own hands. *Finally.*

He kissed her like a starving man. And she was just as hungry. Just as desperate.

She felt the world tilt and spin, more than usual when he was near, and he was lifting her up, pulling her legs around his waist, then taking her mouth again.

As if she was his in every possible way.

And she exulted in it. She loved the hardness of his strong, callused hand against her cheek, giving him total control over the depth and fire of the kiss. His other hand was hot and delicious against her bottom, holding her against the hardest part of him, making her feel shivery and glazed with heat. She loved the thrust of his tongue, the press of his lips, the way he teased and took in turn. He stood there like a rock, holding her so easily, as if she was made of something as insubstantial as cotton, and that made her tremble all the more.

He was so massive. So incontrovertibly male. Sinew and muscle like marble, as if he'd been carved from stone, and yet he was so hot to the touch. *So hot.*

He began to walk, still kissing her with all of that intensity, all of that insistent fire, and she was aware of only a jumble of things around her as he carried her into his house. There was blue everywhere—endless sky and sea through the glass on all sides, a huge abstract painting on a whitewashed wall. Wide-open rooms in that sleek modern style with unusual pops of color here and there.

But mostly she saw that hard face of his, taut with the same mad desire she felt eating her alive. Then everything shifted again and she was flat on her back on some kind of soft white rug near a fireplace that dominated one stark wall, and he was coming down over her with the kind of fluid ease and heart-stopping masculine grace that reminded her, forcefully, that his body was a sleek machine under his command, and he could make it do anything he wished.

Anything at all.

He stretched out beside her, running one of his hands down the length of her slowly, as if claiming her. Learning her. A languorous sweep from the side of one breast to the indentation of her waist, over the curve of her hip, then down the outside of her leg. It was like being bathed in lightning; electrified. One searing burst then another, the voltage of it jolting through her, making her close her eyes against the madness of this. The insanity.

He whispered that phrase again. *"Milaya moya."*

"I don't think I want to know what that means," she whispered, hardly recognizing her own voice when she heard it, so glutted was it with the wildness inside of her, the riot of the storm he'd raised. The storm that showed no sign of easing.

When she opened her eyes, she met his. Black, searing hot—and she trembled at the passion there. The stark sensual intent.

"Sweet." His voice was a rasp in the quiet room. Like a touch all its own, another devastating caress. Something moved across his face then, almost like a kind of anguish, then was gone. "It means 'my sweet.'"

And then he took her mouth again, demanding and possessive, and it was long moments before she realized that as he did, he was also lifting up her dress. He tugged it above her knees. Then up to her waist. The cool air moved over her flushed skin and she froze. Reality trickled back in, and with it, a sudden sharp pang of uneasiness.

"Ivan—"

But his hand was on the bare skin of her thigh, so hot, so possessive. The storm inside her raged on, and she bit her lip. Ivan shifted and looked down at her, his clever eyes searching hers.

Slowly, inexorably, his hand moved higher. He held her gaze. Watching. Waiting.

Miranda's breath sawed in and out. Raw. Almost painful. But she didn't say a word. She didn't tell him to stop. She couldn't seem to form a single syllable. It was as if he'd shorted out her brain.

His hand crept higher and he shifted again, moving down over her with that surprising, distracting grace of his, until he kissed her thigh, right next to where his hand rested, so close to the very heart of her need.

"Ivan." It was so hard to speak. It was so hard to *feel* all of this, to feel it and not simply pass out from the pleasure. Or the deeper emotion she wasn't equipped to handle. Or the rising panic she was struggling to ignore. She didn't know how to feel this much—how to handle this kind of passion, this storm. "I don't…"

"You don't what?"

He was licking her skin, tracing a lazy path of fire along her thigh, and even as she registered the fact that he was pushing her legs apart and settling himself between them, he was there. He threw a single dark look at her, black like silk and as effortlessly seductive, intently sexual, deliciously male, and then pressed his mouth against her, hard.

As if she wasn't wearing that tiny scrap of satin between her legs at all. As if she was already naked.

Miranda arched against him, up off the floor, the pleasure like a shock wave, coursing through her, setting her alight. She felt him in her breasts, her toes. Her skin seemed to burst into flames. He curved his hands around her bottom, holding her to him, taking her. Simply *taking* her as if she'd always been his.

She couldn't understand how he could wreck her like this—how he could make her feel such huge, unwieldy things, so big they were crowding her out of her own body, so giant she could hardly breathe, love and lust and electric *want*—

"I don't—"

But she was panting with that terrible, impossible need and her own slick, hot response, and he simply moved her panties out of his way, then licked his way into the center of her, where she was already molten hot and he seemed to know intuitively exactly how to drive her wild.

Exactly how to make her body arch up again, her entire being focused on the sheer mastery of that hard, perfect mouth, the things that he could do, the *things* that he was *doing*—

It was too much. It was overload. Chaos. She felt strung out, lit up. How could she survive this much pleasure and still be herself? How could she be sure she would live through this at all? How could anything feel this good?

"I don't like—"

"This?"

He did something new with his mouth, licked into her harder. Deeper. She heard a far-off scream of pleasure almost too acute to bear and only dimly understood she'd made it.

"Or this?"

He slid two long, hard fingers deep into the core of her, as if he already knew all of her secrets, as if he'd already had her a thousand times.

And Miranda writhed beneath him, mindless, unable to do anything at all but feel it coming toward her, this wildness like a terror in her veins, her flesh. This impossible crisis, inexorable and his to command. Just as she was.

"I can't—" she began.

"You can. I promised."

And then he took the heat of her in his mouth again, performed that magic that was only his and threw her straight over the edge of the world.

That was one promise kept, Ivan thought with deep male satisfaction as she shuddered in his arms and he had to restrain himself from simply sliding into her then and there, putting the proper end to all of this torture.

God, the ways he wanted her. He was man enough to admit, here, while she still shook herself apart in his arms, that he had wanted her long before he'd met her. That he had entertained any number of fantasies about that snooty little frown of hers that meant that overeducated brain of hers was working overtime, that entrancing sweep of dark red hair that begged for his hands, that beautiful mouth of hers that criticized him so resolutely and was so hot and wild on his.

He had barely begun to scratch the surface of those fantasies. And he was running out of time.

But he wanted her with him, every step of the way. He wanted her fully aware of it when he took her, every inch and every thrust, not blissed out with what he was fairly certain, with no little smugness, was her very first orgasm.

A feeling wholly new to him moved through him then as he looked down at her. He couldn't recognize it. He wasn't sure he cared to. She still breathed so heavily. Her eyes were still shut tight, her face flushed red. She was making the slightest, smallest sound; it was so close to a moan, and it made him want her even more.

He settled himself beside her, propping himself up on his elbow and drew her name on the bare skin of her arm in Russian. *Milaya moya.* His from the start, little though she might know it. And despite what was to come.

But when her eyes finally opened, that dark jade gone green, she looked distressed. Panicked. And when she focused on him, she went pale.

"No," she said, but her voice was strained. Choked.

She pushed against him wildly and he let her go at once, going perfectly still as she rolled and then scrambled away from him. She threw herself back against the nearest bright white couch, her dark red hair and black dress a punch of color against the pale cushions, the stark room; poignant and loud. She tugged her dress down to cover her legs and then she pulled her knees up to her chest and hugged herself.

Like a scared child, not like the woman he knew. Not his bold, fearless professor, who had never met an opponent she couldn't argue down, no matter how foolhardy that argument might be.

"Miranda." He made his voice calm. Soothing. "What is the matter? There is nothing to be afraid of here."

"This can't happen," she said in a heartbreakingly small voice, that was not in any way hers, and then she buried her head against her knees.

A dark suspicion uncurled inside of him, making him deeply, almost incapacitatingly furious. At himself. Her insistence on the separation of mind and body. Her bloodless previous relationships, all talk and so little sex. Her hatred of what he stood for from afar, her stunned, uncertain fascination with him in person. The way she kissed him, as if she couldn't believe he was real, as if she'd never felt anything like it before.

As if some part of her was afraid. Ivan seethed. How had he managed to overlook that? But he knew. He'd been focused on the game. And that glorious heat, that want. That incandescent fire. On having her, not reading her as he should have.

He forced himself to breathe, to focus. To concentrate on here, now. Miranda.

"But it's already happened," he said quietly. "And here we are, all in one piece. Safe."

"Ruined," she whispered, more to her legs than to him, but he heard her all the same, and it felt like a sucker punch, hard and fast to the back of the head, taking him down to his knees. "You've ruined me."

"I don't have that power, *Milaya*," he told her, not permitting his voice to betray a single shred of the fury that roiled inside of him. The fury or the deep sympathy he wished he could express in more than just a few paltry words in his third language. "And neither does anyone else."

He heard a sound that was like a sob, and it broke what was left of his useless old heart into a thousand pieces. He pulled himself up into sitting position, but he didn't go to her, though every part of him wanted to. He watched her delicate head, bent over her knees. Watched her lithe body shake slightly. Listened to the way she breathed, ragged and shallow. And he waited.

Outside, the afternoon wore on. The light thinned, the shadows began to form. The wind picked up, making the palm trees dance slightly. And still he waited.

Eventually, she lifted her head, her face wet with tears and her eyes, those beautiful, defiant eyes, too wide and much too troubled. He hated it. He wanted her dark, clever jade. He wanted that green flash of outrage, that dazed black of passion. Not this.

"This is all I have," she told him, her voice harsh and tight with emotion. She brought up one hand and held it against her forehead, the side of her face, indicating the whole of her head as if she was no more than a brain in a jar. "This is *all* I have. I can't… I don't…"

"You did."

Her eyes streaked to his, and she swallowed hard. "You don't understand."

"Then tell me."

"How can you think this is safe, Ivan? You're the least safe person I could possibly imagine—"

"I keep having to remind you that I am widely considered to be the greatest fighter of all time," he said, cutting her off, his gaze intent on hers. "I still train every day with my brother, who did things so secret and so terrible in the Russian army that they dare not speak his name aloud. And I could beat him with my eyes closed." He let that sink in. Then continued in the same quiet tone. "This is what I do. There is no power on this earth that can get to you through me, Miranda. Not one."

She looked away, out across the vast living room toward the sea that glimmered through the glass walls on three sides. That deep, brooding Pacific blue. Ivan thought he'd lost her, and he couldn't understand the way that felt, the things that surged in him, outraged and very nearly frantic at the very idea. He refused to accept that he couldn't reach her, couldn't help her. That whatever had done this to her could best him, too.

He refused to think about all the reasons why he shouldn't be reacting this way. About how he was supposed to be breaking her apart, not building her back up.

Breathe, he ordered himself, and it took a lifetime of training, of battles hard won, to simply do it. To let her gather herself, swipe her hair back from her face and then begin to speak, as if she was talking to the ocean and he wasn't there at all.

"He beat all of us," she said in a low voice. "My mother. My brother. Me. We all lived in terror of setting off one of his moods, of triggering one of his rages, and it didn't occur to me until much later, when I escaped, that there was no behavior good enough to please him—that he couldn't be pleased, ever. That he *wanted* to do the things he did, or he would have stopped. He didn't stop. He never stopped."

"Your father," Ivan indicated when she didn't, and wondered why he'd imagined that money protected anyone from anything. When people remained people, and bullies remained bullies. He should know. He'd fought so hard to get away from his uncle only to find the world was filled with monsters just like him.

She nodded jerkily, still staring out the windows, her pretty face haunted.

"He was the most physical man I knew," she whispered. "He was so *big*. He broke things with his hands. And he was always *touching* me. My head, my back, my arms—little reminders when we were out in public. That no matter how many times he smiled in church or joked around while he was coaching my brother's soccer games, he could turn on us in an instant. And he did."

Ivan still didn't speak. She turned to face him then, her dark eyes searching his face as if looking for something. Disbelief? Pity? He didn't know, and so he only gazed back at her, knowing nothing showed on his face but calm, easy compassion, no matter how it killed him to stay so quiet when what he wanted to do was find whoever had done this to her, the man who should have loved her the most, and break him into pieces. With his own big hands.

"I had one date," she told him, her voice a painful little whisper in the quiet room. "I was sixteen. I'd decided early on that there was only one way out of there, and I was determined to take it. I studied like a maniac. I skipped two grades in school. But there was this boy." Her smile was so sad it made his heart twist hard in his chest. "We saw a movie the week after we graduated from high school. He drove me home in his car and then he kissed me. It was my first. I forgot myself completely." She pressed her lips together, hugged her legs tighter to her torso. "And when I walked into the house, my father called me a whore and beat me up so badly I had to stay in bed for three weeks."

Ivan couldn't help the sound he made then. He shook his head when she looked at him, so very carefully, as if she was waiting for him to turn on her. Which, of course, she was. *And you will in the end, won't you?* a small voice inside of him asked. *If you keep to the plan…* But he shoved that aside.

"You are not talking about a *man*, Miranda," he said quietly. "You must know this. A creature who would do such things is the worst kind of coward. My uncle was the very same sort."

"But you fought him." Her voice was bitter. A slap of pain, of self-recrimination. "You stood up to him."

"I was six feet by the time I was twelve. What do you imagine you could have done? What use would fighting have been to you when he could break your bones? Where was your brother?"

She shook her head, her eyes a misery, and again, it hurt him not to reach for her, not to try to soothe her with his hands—as if that would help.

"At my college graduation, I was ready for them," she said after a moment. She swiped at her eyes with the backs of her hands. "I'd been accepted into my graduate program. I had housing, a stipend. A job to help pay the bills. So I finally stood up to him." Her eyes swam with tears. "I told him he was an abusive bully who'd made all our lives hell and I wanted nothing more to do with him. I thought my mother and my brother would applaud."

Ivan sighed, knowing where this was going. "Miranda…"

"My father walked out of the restaurant," she said very precisely, as if careful enunciation might keep her from crying. "I thought my mother would choose me but instead she told me I was dead to her, and I haven't spoken to either of them since." She let out a sound too hollow to be a laugh, and a tear traced a sluggish path down her cheek. "My brother thinks I'm delusional. He sends me hateful emails when he sees me on television. He thinks I need a strong hand to keep me in my place. I got a few messages from him when I was in New York and guess what? He thinks you can do the job nicely."

Ivan sat forward slightly, and waited until her eyes met his.

"Come here," he said. Very quietly.

She shivered, and not entirely in fear, he

thought. But then she shook her head, tears swimming in her eyes again.

"I can't. I just can't. You make me…" She dragged a hand through her hair, scraping her hair back from her face. "You make me forget myself again, and I can't, Ivan. *I can't.*"

"You can." He opened up his hands and laid them, palms up, on his knees. "Just as soon as it occurs to you that you have already said far nastier things to me and about me than you have ever said to a man like your father, and I have yet to harm you in any way. Just as soon as that marvelous brain of yours analyzes what that means. What it suggests about how safe you are here. With me."

"Ivan—"

"I have very strong hands," he said in the same tone, flipping them over on his knees, then back, inviting her to study them. "I've spent my entire life studying fighting. I have black belts in three martial arts systems. I've won every MMA championship I ever entered. You think that makes me more violent, more dangerous, than the average man?"

"Of course it does. It would have to."

"You're wrong."

She didn't like that, clearly, but she shifted position against the white couch, dropping her knees to the side and no longer hugging herself in that way, as if she was protecting herself from a blow. Her eyes moved over his hands, then back to his face.

"The more I train, the more I learn, the less I fight," he said quietly. "The less I have to fight."

He watched her take that in, start to think about it. He felt a trickle of relief when he saw that frown of hers again, carving that familiar line between her brows. This was the Miranda he knew. This was his Professor.

He told himself that was only relief he felt. Nothing more. Nothing deeper, more dangerous.

"Come here," he said again, softer this time.

"I don't think I want to."

"I think you do."

He still didn't move, and after a very long time, when the sun began to sink into vibrant golds and reds across the wide horizon and the house lights came on around them, low and warm, she exhaled a long and shuddering breath. And then, very slowly, very carefully, she moved back toward him across the polished wood floor. She stopped when she was directly in front of him, and knelt there, frightened eyes big in her delicate face.

He indicated the hands he still held there, open on his knees, and she swallowed convulsively. She took another deep breath. Then she reached out and placed her hands in his, one after the other, her fingers cold and stiff. He closed his fingers over hers carefully. Slowly. Giving her ample chance to pull away.

"I'd fight your demons for you, Professor," he whispered. "But they'd put me in jail."

She trembled, but she didn't pull away.

"I thought my old boyfriends were bad at sex," she whispered in a rush, not looking at him. "But it wasn't them, was it? It was me. There's something wrong with me. He— I'm ruined."

"You're perfect," he told her very distinctly. "And you're safe with me. I promise you."

She shook her head, but she didn't move her hands, and they were warming against his, her skin heating from the contact with his. She didn't seem to notice that she was also breathing more steadily, more easily, breath by breath. That he was calming her with his touch.

"You don't know that," she said after a moment,

looking down at the floor. "Look what happened today."

"Look at me." His voice was commanding then. Sure. Her head jerked up but she met his gaze. He felt her shiver slightly, and he didn't let go. "I'm not a teenage boy or a coward. I told you. I can control myself. You can't hurt me. And I won't hurt you."

He squeezed her hands slightly in his when she began to make a face, and her gaze slid back to his, reluctantly. So reluctantly, and he saw the fear there. And more than that, the hope. It moved in him, shaming him. Making him wish for things he knew he'd never have all over again. Making him wish they were different people. Making him wish they'd met a different way, played a different game.

And as she stared back at him, that terrible tension draining from her face little by little, her skin becoming less pale, looking more and more like Miranda by the moment, he told himself that it was true. That he could keep that promise, despite what he had to do.

That he would.

But then she tilted her head forward and kissed him.

CHAPTER TEN

MIRANDA didn't let herself think. There'd been enough of that.

She simply kissed him again and again, angling her mouth over his the way he'd taught her, and it was sweet and right and then, once more, that fire.

That wild, unquenchable fire that, she understood now, had always been leading her here. To him. The only man who made her burn. Who made her *want* to burn. Who she believed would keep her safe no matter what happened when she was nothing more than ash. Who might even fight off her nightmares, if she let him.

Hadn't he just proved it?

He pulled back, though he didn't move his hands, and she knew, somehow, that he was afraid of scaring her off again. It made her heart kick hard against her ribs. Then ache.

"You don't have to kiss me," he said, frowning slightly.

She wanted to sob. It felt like she might—or simply explode all around him, and neither one was what she wanted. So she took refuge in her favorite suit of armor.

"Of course I don't have to." She raised her brows at him. "That would be coercive and repellent. Much like our public displays of feigned affection."

He watched her for a long moment. Then blinked. For a breath, Miranda thought he might force her back into the fragile space she could still feel all around them, clinging to them—that he might say something else so devastatingly perfect, so miraculously *right*, that she would collapse before him all over again—

"Yes," he said, the rich rumble of his mocking voice moving through her, like a shiver, his dark eyes shrewd as they tracked over her face, then down to where she gripped his hands too tightly—and didn't let go. "I noted how repelled you were. It was your defining characteristic in all of those tabloid pictures."

This time, she felt that sardonic lash like the gift it was.

"Ivan." She waited for those midnight eyes to slide to hers again. So guarded as they searched hers, as if he was waiting for her to dissolve into sobs all over again, despite her brusque tone of voice. "Be quiet."

His dark eyes gleamed.

And when she leaned in to take his mouth again, he didn't say a word. He only kissed her back. Long and sweet. Endless. Heat spiraled into pleasure and rolled through her, making the body so recently racked in such old anguish begin to hum again. As if he was making her brand-new.

Miranda was the one who wanted more, who pulled her hands from his to hold his face between them, that strong, hard jaw scraping gently, erotically beneath her palms. She was the one who moved closer, then closer still, unable to get enough of his taste, his touch, the sheer, dizzying magic of his mouth on hers.

But he still didn't move to hold her, to touch her, and eventually she couldn't take it any longer.

"Why aren't you touching me?" she demanded.

His rare, real smile lit up his face and charmed her straight through to the bone, as he lifted a hand to graze his knuckles over her cheek, like she was somehow precious to him. She wanted to sink into it—into him. She wanted to simply disappear into that smile, that touch.

"I don't want to be another thing that scares you, Miranda." Something moved over his face, like a shadow, but then disappeared so fast she thought she must have imagined it. "No matter what happens."

"I want *you*," she said with quiet conviction. Because she knew that, if nothing else. She knew it in the way she knew that she needed breath to live, and she didn't want to examine that, analyze it. She just wanted him. Maybe she always had. Maybe that was why all of this felt so inevitable. "Not the watered-down version you trot out for the damaged woman who sobbed out a sad story on your floor."

"This is not 'watered down,'" he said, that rich current of laughter in his voice then, and flirting with that hard mouth. "This is patient. I'm not at all surprised you can't recognize it."

"You look at me and make me think you'll burn me alive where I stand," she whispered, not caring if it made her seem needy, desperate. Not caring about anything but the way she knew he could touch her—the way she wanted him to touch her. The way he'd simply…swept her up, from the first moment she'd met him. "That's what I want, Ivan. I don't want you to treat me like…like I'm ruined."

"You already think I'm a wild, untamed animal," he pointed out bluntly, though that gleam in his eyes was brighter. Hotter. It made her flush. Squirm slightly where she knelt before him. "Why would I want to go and do something that will inevitably prove it to you?"

"I don't think you're an animal," she retorted, and as she said it, she realized that it was true. And that she hadn't thought anything of the kind in a long time. It was astonishing. Dizzying. And it meant a whole host of things she didn't want to think about. Not here. Not now. She slammed the door shut on all of them and looked at him instead.

"A caveman," he continued in that same blunt voice, as if he knew what she was thinking and didn't care. "A Neanderthal. Testosterone-poisoned."

"I said all of those things, yes." Miranda searched his face, which he kept perfectly blank. But she knew better. She knew he was fighting back the same desire that was coursing through her, making her burn all over again every time she inhaled. She could sense it like some kind of aura that surrounded them both. "Don't tell me this is your revenge. I called you a caveman and so now you're going to act like a Victorian maiden?"

"Yes." But his other hand moved then, tracing a lazy line up the length of her spine, making her turn molten hot, making goose bumps break out over her arms. "I plan to punish you with luke-warm, perfectly competent sex."

By the time he finished the sentence his hand had made it to the nape of her neck, and he left it there, a hot, hard, delicious weight. A kind of sensual promise. She shivered against it, into it, and that crook in the corner of his hard mouth deepened.

"I've already had that," she reminded him, breathlessly. "I've *only* had that."

He smiled again, and it was far wickeder this time, and seemed to shoot off sparks inside of her that flipped into explosions and made her belly tighten around that same deep, low ache that she understood, now, only he could ease.

"And what do I do when my vastly superior touch renders you a sobbing mess on my floor yet again, as it inevitably will?" he asked gently, his tone teasing. He traced a feather-light pattern along her cheek again, then over her lips, then down to her collarbone, bathing her in light. In yearning. "I am, in fact, that good."

It was, Miranda realized as she blinked back the heat behind her eyes, the nicest thing this man—any man—had ever done for her. Made her feel normal. Made her feel…unruined. As if she wasn't damaged at all.

"Do I have to beg you to prove it?" she asked, her voice catching.

"I believe I told you that one day, you would."

"I don't know how to beg," she said, her pulse rocketing in her veins as his dark gaze moved to her mouth. "I was hoping you could teach me that, too."

"Miranda, Miranda." He sighed. "You are far too educated already."

And then, finally, *finally*, he took control.

He simply picked her up. He slid his hands beneath her arms and lifted her, settling her astride his lap. He was so strong. She watched the play of his muscles, the sheer power he demonstrated so casually, and knew that when she began to tremble this time, it was not from fear.

He gazed up at her for a brief, searing moment, and then he claimed her mouth.

And this time, the fire roared. It swept through Miranda, making her melt and burn and melt again. She collapsed against the hard wall of his glorious chest, and sighed at the searing friction they made. And it wasn't close enough.

She felt desperate, needy, and rocked herself against the hard proof of his desire until he groaned. He tangled one hand in her hair to hold her head precisely where he wanted it, and moved to press kisses along her cheek, her neck, then pulled back to reach between them and, in a single sweep of his arm, tug her dress up and over her head.

Miranda was sure her heartbeat was loud enough to drown out the world. She couldn't seem to do more than catch shallow breaths, and everything seemed to stop as Ivan stared down at her, as if mesmerized by what he'd uncovered. She felt that low ache inside of her pull tight, and shuddered, so much closer to that wild oblivion he'd showed her than should have been possible.

"Ti takaya krasivaya," he muttered, in reverent tones, and then he pressed his mouth to the hollow between her breasts, where the cups of

her pale blue bra met in a delicate bow. "You're beautiful. Perfect."

And in that moment, she believed him.

Miranda arched against him, into him. Her blood seemed to sing inside of her, her head spun, and she was only dimly aware of the way he held her with one arm and even so, managed to unclasp her bra. She helped as he pulled it from her arms and tossed it aside. But she knew nothing else when he fastened his dangerous mouth to one taut nipple, pulling it into all of that wicked heat.

He started to speak in Russian, a low, rough music to her ears, as he worked a trail of bright, hot fire from one breast to the other. Then back. As if she was some kind of candy, and he wanted to lick up every last bit of it. She felt the pull of his mouth in her pulse, in her fingers, and like a hungry blaze between her legs.

He moved without warning, shifting them around so that she lay on her back and he was stretched out above her, and for a moment he paused there, suspended on his hands, and Miranda could see the passion etched hard into his features. It made him look stark. Fierce. She thought he was beautiful, too.

"This time," he said, "when you scream, remember that I am right here."

She couldn't speak. She could only nod, and then her heart flipped in her chest when he leaned down to kiss her sweetly.

But it was only the one kiss, and then he turned back to her breasts. He tested their shape in his hands, with his mouth. He licked her until she writhed beneath him, and then he reached down between them and simply held the heat of her in his hand. She bucked against him, dazed with this madness, this sweet, impossible insanity.

"Ivan—" Her voice was cracked. Crazed.

And he ignored her anyway. He used his teeth against one sensitive peak, a gentle if deliberate scrape, while at the same time he pressed his palm hard against the core of her, and once again, Miranda flew apart in a great, shuddering tornado of bliss.

When she came back to herself, he was naked, and so was she. It took one breath to realize that, and another to comprehend that he had settled himself between her legs, the head of him teasing her entrance.

She didn't have time to be afraid. She didn't have time to throw herself across the room again, or cry. He was so big, so hot, and there was that ruthlessness of his that made her weak. It made her want to melt all around him. It made her *want* with parts of herself she'd never known before.

He braced himself on one hand and slid the other around to lift her bottom closer to him. One more breath, ragged and wild. His dark gaze on hers, formidable and dangerous, even now. Especially now.

"I don't want to be ruined," she whispered.

"There is more than one kind of ruin," he said in a gruff, thrilling voice that made her want to bask in him like sunlight. "This is the good kind."

And then he slid into her in one slick, devastating thrust.

She went wild beneath him, and the feel of it, her silky limbs wrapped around him, her soft skin flushed from his mouth and hot to the touch, almost did him in. She arched against him, pressing that lithe body of hers to his in a glorious stretch, and it took everything he had to keep from losing himself there and then.

If he was a good man, a sensitive man, he would

love her softly. Sweetly. Make her come around him again and again, languorous and endless.

But he wasn't that man, and anyway, she didn't want the watered-down version of him. She wanted the real him. All of him. Ivan didn't think she could know how that had exploded inside of him. What it meant. He wasn't sure he wanted to think about it himself. He bent his head to hers, burying his face in the sweet hollow of her neck and shoulder, and set the demanding rhythm his body craved.

And she met it. Threw back her head and gloried in it.

Which made him that much crazier.

She wrapped her arms around his neck, pressing those maddeningly perfect breasts into his chest. She nearly undid him. She was hot and soft and melting all around him, and he was desperate for her. For this.

I will never get enough, he thought very distinctly.

He heard her small, erotic moans in his ear and turned his head to capture that mouth of hers again.

There were no games here, in this meeting of tongues and lips. As the fire that burned through them seared them both, reducing them both to nothing more than dancing flames. And still he moved in her, filled with her in ways he couldn't begin to explore, mad with need, wild with delight at her perfect, slick fit.

Mine, he thought when she grew taut against him, when her fingers dug into his skin and her eyes closed tight. *Mine*, he thought when he reached between them and found the center of desire, making her cry out his name before she hurtled once more over that cliff.

All mine, he thought, when at last he followed her over the edge, her own name like an answered prayer on his lips.

This was what *shifting* felt like, Miranda told herself the next morning, when she woke and realized there had been no nightmares. That he'd wiped them away, or helped her face them at long last. Or perhaps it was that she'd done the actual shifting some time ago, and this was what happened afterward. Either way, she was lost.

Wholly, unutterably lost, but she couldn't find it anywhere in her to mind. There was that little whisper of warning that moved in her, dark and distracting, but she didn't listen to it. She couldn't.

There was only Ivan. At last.

"I—" she'd begun in that heady rush of the forty-eight precious hours that followed that first night, leading up to the premiere she'd come to California to attend. "I think I..."

But she couldn't finish. She couldn't quite say it.

"I told you I was good, Professor," he replied with that casual arrogance that made her smile, stretched out across the massive bed in his minimalistic bedroom, with nothing to soften its modern, masculine edges but the Pacific Ocean just beyond the walls of glass. Nothing to interrupt the fact of his magnificence, his perfectly honed body displayed like treasure on the sumptuously dark brown sheets.

She was sprawled across his chest, overcome with all these *things* she felt. They were cracking her wide open, making her question everything. She traced the three letters tattooed over his heart.

"What does this say?"

"*Mir,*" he said gruffly. A guarded look in his eyes. "It's the Russian word for *peace.*"

Her eyes filled up, her own heart ached for him, and he took her hand away from the tattoo. She remembered the balcony in Cap Ferrat, when he'd spoken of a better way to fight.

"Do not make mountains from molehills," he ordered her.

"Relax," she'd replied, hurt when she shouldn't have been. Just because she'd shifted into this other, more emotional place, it didn't mean he had. It didn't mean he would. She knew she had to come to terms with that. "This is just sex."

He'd pinned her with one of those brooding looks of his then, his eyes so dark it was like nighttime, and something clutched inside of her. He was a fighter with *peace* etched over his heart. He was more alone than anyone she'd ever known—maybe even more than she was, and something in her howled for him.

"As long as it is not insipid sex," he'd said after a long moment. And then he'd pulled her head to his and made her forget again. For a while.

Ivan found himself talking. A lot.

They sat out on a terrace overlooking the sea, the sun falling over them like a caress, and he told her about long, Russian winters that felt as if they'd never end, that stayed in a man's bones even all these years later.

"I like hot places," he said, even smiling. "The hotter and drier the better."

She laughed. "I don't blame you."

They lay in his bed, still panting from another round of the kind of sex that he thought might alter him permanently, and he told her about fighting.

His first championship title fight. What it was like to come to the United States for the first time. How quickly he'd realized that not being fluent in English was as dangerous as not being prepared for a match—that it left him open to attack.

"You make it sound as if you were surrounded by attackers," she said, her fingers moving lazily through his hair.

"I was," he said. "I am. And only sometimes in the ring."

They walked along the edge of his bluff that overlooked the sea and he told her about his little-boy memories of the Soviet Union, and his far sharper and more dangerous memories of what had happened after it fell, when he was only ten and forced to grow up. Fast. How he'd lost his parents and gained his uncle. How he'd had nothing to do with all of his fear and pain and anger but fight. For his life. For Nikolai's.

"That must have been terrifying," she said, frowning out at the ocean as if she was glaring at his past. "Not just losing your parents, but your whole way of life. Your whole world in one year."

"It made me who I am today," he replied, his voice harder than necessary, almost as if she'd forced him to discuss this when he knew full well she hadn't. He could not seem to keep himself from her. She had asked for the unwatered-down version, and he wanted to give it to her—a wholly new and unfamiliar urge. "For good or ill."

He heard the little sigh she gave then, despite the breeze that lifted the ends of her dark red hair and made it seem to glow in the sunlight.

"Do you think we'll spend the rest of our lives cleaning up the mess?" she asked softly. "When it wasn't even our mess?"

He knew what she meant. "I think the past informs everything we do. Ghosts are with us, whether we acknowledge them or not."

She glanced back over her shoulder at the house, then looked at him, her dark jade gaze troubled.

"Like your brother."

He felt that jolt in him, and questioned again why he was doing this. Why he was sharing anything at all with her, much less these particular things. Much less *himself*, when he'd never told any of this to women he'd been genuinely dating from the start. There was so little time left. He had accomplished what he'd set out to do. He'd seduced her. Their fake relationship was established. All that was left was the very public, hopefully televised dumping, which would render her mute. At last.

He should have been oozing triumph from every pore. He certainly shouldn't have been sharing his private business. His private pain.

But he couldn't seem to help himself.

He turned slightly and saw what she must have—Nikolai out on one of the higher balconies, arms crossed, watching. Always watching. He could feel his brother's typical disapproval like its own, stiff breeze.

"If my brother is a ghost," he said quietly, "the fault is mine."

She only looked at him curiously, as if the guilt that was so much a part of him didn't make any sense.

"I left him," Ivan choked out. "To the tender mercies of our uncle. He escaped into the military when he could, and he thought so little of himself that he volunteered for a unit that took chunks of his soul every time he went on a mission. For a time he thought he could drink what he was missing back in, but that didn't work. His wife left him. She took his child. He lost everything."

"He hasn't lost you."

Ivan didn't know what twisted in him, rolling over like an earthquake, shaking things loose that he hadn't known could move. For a moment he thought the whole world shifted—this was California, after all—but Miranda still stood there, looking up at him, so pretty in something flowing and red that teased over her body to skim her thighs. So it was only him, and he didn't know what that meant, or how to handle it.

"You don't know what you're talking about," he said, because he had no idea what was happening, and trying to cram it back down where it belonged seemed like the best course of action. "It's my fault he was put in the position of having to make those decisions. If I'd stayed—"

"You would have had to make the same decisions that he did," she interrupted him with a shrug. "Just as he could have followed your example, presumably. If he didn't, that's sad, but it's not your fault."

Ivan said nothing. He was, he thought in some astonishment, incapable of speech. That thing in him shook harder. Seismic overload, turning everything to rubble. Cities collapsing. Landscapes changing. He was surprised he didn't fall to the ground.

Miranda looked at him, then frowned in concern. She reached over and put her hand on his arm, and he had the strangest sensation, then— that this small, slight woman was holding him up. That she could carry him, if she wanted. If he let her.

"Ivan," she said gently. Insistently, her gaze never leaving his, and causing, he realized, the same kind of trouble all through him. He should have taken precautions. He should have listened to his brother. He should have paid more attention to what she was doing to him—because now, he was very much afraid, it was far too late. "You do know that, don't you?"

The red carpet for Ivan's Jonas Dark premiere didn't overwhelm Miranda this time. She didn't care about the cameras. She didn't care about the roar of the crowd or the attempts at intrusive questions. She was aware of nothing but Ivan. She saw the way he looked at her that was only theirs. All of the stories he'd told her, all the ways he'd shared himself, as if he wanted to be as open to her as she was to him… It made her imagine he was not as alone as he sometimes seemed.

Or that she wasn't.

She was dressed in the shimmering blue dress she'd worn as little more than fabric in that dressing room in Paris. It clung to her breasts and then fell like water to the floor, reminding her somehow of the sea. The back was a wide V, allowing him to brush her skin with his fingertips whenever he liked, catapulting them both back to Paris. To what could have been.

"Do you know what I wanted to do to you the last time you wore this?" he asked, murmuring into her ear as they entered the theater.

"I wanted you to do it," she told him, smiling. "I dreamed about it for nights on end."

"Lucky for you this is Hollywood," he replied, that fire in dark gaze. "Where all your wildest dreams can come true."

And he was as good as his word.

He didn't wait for them to go back to his Malibu house. The moment they entered the limousine that was to take them from the premiere to the after-party, he pulled her to him.

"No kissing," he told her sternly, making her melt with the heat lurking in his voice and gleaming in his gaze. "We have to look presentable."

He simply picked her up and settled her over his lap. He moved her skirts out of the way, and pulled her panties to the side as he worked his own fly. And then, his hands deliciously hard on her hips, he thrust deep into her, made them both sigh with that sheer, dizzying pleasure that was only theirs.

Only him, she thought. *Only Ivan.*

He gazed up at her then, and showed her that smile that she understood then that she would do anything to see. Anything at all. Especially this.

"You'll have to do all the work." It was a dare. A challenge.

And she met it.

The car slid through the streets of Hollywood. Miranda could see lights, other cars, city life clogging the roads and surging up and down the sidewalks—and all the while, Ivan was so hard beneath her and inside of her. So deliciously hard.

She reached up and braced on hand against the roof of the car, and the other on his shoulder. And then she began to move.

It was so good. It felt like glory and wild, slick heat, perfect and impossible all at once.

She moved faster, making him groan. He let his head fall back against the seat and she watched him as she rocked against him, into him, circling her hips instinctively, finding the best fit, the hottest angle. He was so fierce, so intensely masculine, so ruthlessly physical, even with his eyes closed. Even as he let her take some kind of control. It made her feel wild with a new kind of power, incandescent with it. With him. Like she was made to do this. Like it made her new, and strong. That she could reduce this tough, hard man to nothing more than need.

That she could make him come.

And then fling herself over the edge behind him, knowing he would be there on the other side of all of this wildness to catch her, every time.

She had originally intended to go back to New York after the premiere, to wait out her time between Ivan's events in the comfort and privacy of her own home. But after the premiere, sometime so far into the night that it was already the next morning, she woke to find him holding her close, his face buried against her neck.

"What's the matter?" she asked, her hands going to his face, his back.

But he didn't answer.

He entered her slowly. As if it was sacred. He moved like liquid; gentle, inexorable. He loved her with his mouth, his hands, making her writhe beneath him in that same quiet, shattering way. As if he was imprinting himself on her—making her his as surely as if he'd branded her. Because she understood that there was no way she would ever survive this—*him*—intact. No way she could even attempt it.

And when he lifted his face to hers, she could see that he wanted that.

As if this was his way of saying the things that couldn't be said.

This beautiful, impossible wave of sensation, pulling them both up and then crashing them down, until they collapsed against each other, tangled and breathless, wrapped up in his bed like they were a knot that could never be untied.

And so she didn't leave for New York the next

day, as she'd planned. She just…stayed. And promised herself she'd love him as long as he'd let her.

One afternoon she sat on one of the terraces and watched as Ivan and his brother trained in their deadly sport on that bluff high above the sea. She'd wrapped herself in one of Ivan's button-down shirts, letting herself indulge in the sensation of being held by him when he wasn't near her. She'd woken from the usual daze he'd left her in to find him gone from his bed, and had followed the odd sounds on the breeze to this terrace.

She knew she should be disgusted. Appalled. But she wasn't.

It didn't look like jocks gone wrong. It didn't look like cavemen. It looked like some kind of beautiful, lethal dance. Art on the edge of a blade. They circled each other, came together, flipped and kicked and rolled. They were like two titans, all muscle and grace, and she was most struck by the identical expressions on their hard, Korovin faces.

That fierce concentration. That deadly intent.

And the joy.

Pure and unadulterated.

Miranda found herself swallowing, hard, against a lump in her throat. She had to look away. She didn't have to be told that these were men for whom joy was an intellectual exercise, not a fact. Not something they'd experienced much of—but they experienced it here. In the display of their magnificent skill. In this dance that only a very few people in the world could do as well as they did.

This is the good kind of ruin, Ivan had told her. He'd meant sex. Allowing herself to fall apart in his arms without fearing the consequences. But she knew that it went much further than that— that it was, at the end of the day, a kind of warning it was much too late to heed.

She knew, with a certainty that she'd never felt before, about anything, that this time with him had changed everything. Had altered her, profoundly and fundamentally. She would never be the same, and there was a part of her that welcomed that.

She was in love with him.

And she was going to have to find a way to survive that, because the Korovin Foundation Benefit was coming closer by the day, and there was no reason to suppose this would ever go further than that. Nor that it should, no matter how she felt. No matter what she hoped, deep inside.

After all, they'd agreed.

CHAPTER ELEVEN

EVERYTHING was perfect.

Nikolai gave his first speech as president of the Korovin Foundation, making it clear that he was fully capable of ushering the charity into its bright new future, his ruthless coldness seeming more like pure, corporate focus when he spoke. Ivan gave his own speech afterward, using a highly sterilized account of his childhood to explain why he wanted to take the gifts he'd been given from the ring and from the screen and find a way to help children in need. So they didn't have to choose between their self-respect and their survival. So they could choose to fight because they wanted to fight, not because they had no other way. So they could avoid selling themselves, whether to fight promoters or militaries or the far more unsavory "saviors" they might encounter in their times of need.

So they could choose.

All the while Miranda stood next to him, glowing like the trophy he'd once told her she wasn't, gleaming and unutterably beautiful. Her hair was coiled back into a complicated twist of braids and pins that looked somehow effortlessly chic. Her eyes were mysterious. And she wore very high, very delicate silver shoes that made her look tall, invincible and deeply, deeply sexy. Every inch the Greenwich, Connecticut, heiress she would have been, had her life taken a different path. Had her father been something other than a monster.

Her final dress from the Parisian couture house was one of their signature creations, understated yet proud. Ivan had loved the sketches—had, in fact, spent longer than necessary imagining her in the dress—but the reality was far better than his fantasies. The dress managed to be bold and elegant at once, a deceptively simple-looking near-silver concoction that fit so beautifully it made her look edible. A smart, sexy package he couldn't seem to get enough of.

And it was different, somehow, that she knew the truth about him. All of his truths. The stark terror he'd lived through, the guilt he couldn't help but feel for escaping so much sooner than Nikolai had. She knew everything, and still she looked at him in that way of hers, as if he was something miraculous, after all: a good man.

And because of that, it felt like less of a performance. Less of an act. It felt real.

Just as she did. Her hand in his, their fingers laced together.

He didn't know how he would let her go. He couldn't imagine it—but then, how could this go on? How many of his internal foundations would she shatter before she was done?

He realized, looking at her there on the small dais the event managers had erected in the corner of the ballroom he usually used as his dojo, that she was the only fight he didn't think he could win.

That he didn't *want* to win. He just wanted her.

He didn't have the slightest idea what to do about that. Not when he still owed his brother so much. Not when he'd promised.

"That was wonderful," she told him when all the speeches were done, the formal pictures taken, and there was only the mingling left to do. She smiled at him, and he knew that was real. He knew her now. He could feel her inside of him, like a small, perfect light. Like hope. "I think you made the whole house cry."

"So long as they dry their tears with their checkbooks," he murmured, "we should be fine."

Her smile deepened when he pulled their joined hands to his lips and placed a kiss there.

"I'm sure they will," she said. "Especially if they get a chance to talk to you about it." A curious sort of expression moved over her face, then disappeared behind a new smile he liked a good deal less than the one before. He wanted to know what she was hiding behind it.

"We have things to talk about," he said, trying to see behind her dark jade gaze. He didn't want to share her, he realized. Tonight or ever. He wanted to hide them both away from the world and fall into her, just as he'd been doing since she came to Los Angeles. He wanted that with a sudden surge of fierceness that surprised him. "Tonight."

"Worry about your benefit," she replied, which was completely unsatisfactory.

"Tonight," he repeated more firmly.

"Go," she whispered, and let go of his hand.

He shouldn't have felt it like a loss.

But he had work to do, so he left her side, pasted on his Hollywood smile and got to it.

* * *

This is it, Miranda told herself as she fixed her lipstick in the mirror of the small powder room hidden away in the house's impressive library. *This is the end.*

There was no use pretending otherwise.

Because Ivan had talked a lot. He'd talked about his childhood, about his fighting years, about the foolish things he'd done when he was newly a movie star and could no longer step foot in public without being propositioned and paparazzied. Or both. He'd talked and talked, as if some wall had broken down inside of him.

But he hadn't said anything about this agreement of theirs. He hadn't said that he wanted anything more than what they'd laid out in the documents they'd both signed. He hadn't mentioned it at all—he'd only taken her with an ever-intensifying ferocity, leaving her mindless and spent.

Which said all he meant to say, she supposed. She imagined that was what he wanted to talk about later tonight. The simple mechanics of how this would end.

She would be elegant about it, she decided, pressing her lips together and ignoring the dark shadows in her own eyes. She would pretend she was as sophisticated as he undoubtedly was. She would act the way she imagined that Parisian mistress might have acted centuries ago, upon finding herself summarily dismissed in the same matter-of-fact fashion. She would handle herself with grace and maturity, and save the sobbing for when she was back in New York. Alone.

She could do this.

The clutch handbag she held vibrated, and she sighed, digging into it for her cell phone. It was her literary agent—again. He'd called almost every day for the duration of her time with Ivan, and, she reasoned, she might as well answer him now. She might as well start this terrible ball rolling.

"It's over," she said instead of saying hello. "I assume that's why you've been calling."

He paused for only the tiniest moment. "When you say 'over,'" he said carefully, every inch the placating agent, "exactly what do you mean by that?"

"I mean Ivan and me. We're finished." She stood with the phone to her ear and played with the impossibly decadent fabric of the dress with her free hand. It was sumptuous. It felt decadent and sensual against her skin, the way Ivan did. How was she going to let go of that? "I'm coming home tomorrow without him." She took a breath, squeezed her eyes shut. "And you should know that there isn't going to be any book."

"What happened? You broke up? Maybe you'll get back together—"

"We won't." It was important to sound firm. Unemotional. Maybe her voice would rub off on her heart. And if she faked it long enough, maybe it would come true.

"—and maybe in a few weeks when you're looking at things in a new way, you'll remember that you need a new book idea. Your publisher needs a new book idea. And this one is a guaranteed bestseller. How often does that happen? I'll tell you how often. Never."

"No book," she repeated, emphasizing each word, as if maybe he hadn't heard her the first time.

"Miranda." She could almost see that patented expression he trotted out at moments like this, frowning and concerned. "This is your career."

"Is my career solely dependent on gossiping about Ivan Korovin?" she asked him, and maybe her tone was sharper then than strictly necessary, not that she blamed him for the choices she'd made. That was on her. "Then it isn't much of a career, is it? It's time for something new. Long past time."

"I don't think you've really thought this through—"

"This isn't a negotiation, Bob," she said, fighting to keep the edge out of her voice this time but not sure she succeeded. "I'm not writing another word about Ivan. I'm not talking about him in public ever again. That part of my career is over."

And then she cut off the call.

She expected to feel regret, panic. She expected she might fight the urge to call her agent back at once and tell him she was sorry, overly emotional, made silly by all of this. She thought she should have been gasping for air over a decision she hadn't known she was going to make until she'd opened her mouth and announced it. But instead she only stood there, and she was fine.

Because the least she could do was not be one of his attackers outside the ring. She had to blink hard, then, to keep the sudden heat from spilling over. *The very least you can do is that.*

She squared her shoulders and wrenched open the powder room door—then gasped involuntarily when she saw the figure standing there, just outside. Tall, intimidating. Ice-cold eyes fixed on her in their usual glacial manner.

Nikolai.

She couldn't pretend he didn't make her nervous, but she forced a smile anyway. *Elegant. Sophisticated.* This might have all started with an embarrassing public scene, but it didn't have to end that way. She wouldn't let it.

"I didn't see you there," she said inanely, as if she could have spied him through the door.

His frigid gaze tracked over her face, and she marveled, not for the first time, that he and Ivan could be related. Ivan was all heat. That molten force of his, that simmering, searing power. While Nikolai was all deep frost and drifts of snow, shaped into daggers. She fought off a shiver.

"Come," he ordered her in that unfriendly way of his. "Ivan waits for you."

And it was just like that first night in that Georgetown hotel, she thought as she fell into obedient step behind him. Her very own fearful little symmetry to hold on to, as if it meant something. As if it was some kind of bread-crumb trail that would lead her out of these woods of her own making.

She was such a fool.

But she followed Nikolai even so, out of the kitchen and into the crowd.

And it didn't occur to her until much later that he must have heard every single word of her phone call.

Ivan didn't know how late it was when he felt he'd made the appropriate rounds, posed with all the key donors for more photographs and could look around for Miranda again. He'd seen her earlier, out on the lawn near the pool, shining brighter than the lanterns strung above her like she was her own constellation. It had physically hurt him not to go to her then, touch her, bask in all of that light she threw around so carelessly.

And now, of course, she was nowhere to be found. He found his way out to a secluded corner of the ground-level patio and let himself breathe for a moment near one of the dramatically high cactus arrangements that his landscaper had been so insistent on placing at intervals along the edge of the patio, creating the illusion of private nooks. He gazed out at the moon high over the dark sea, and let the mask of *Ivan Korovin, Famous Actor*, slip just the slightest bit.

"Has the plan changed?" Nikolai asked mildly, coming to stand next to him. "Because if not, you are running out of time."

Ivan felt himself tense and tried to control it. He shouldn't want to punch his own brother in the face. What did that say about him? That he wanted to pick a woman over his own blood?

But he did. And he hated himself for that, too.

"Maybe you have become so immune to any hint of pleasure that you can't hear the sound of the band playing, even now," Ivan said when he was certain he could speak smoothly, easily. "The party is in full swing. There is nothing but time."

"Why didn't you take advantage of the perfect opportunity earlier?" Nikolai asked, almost casually. Almost. If he'd been someone else. "You had a microphone in your hand."

"That would have been an excellent idea," Ivan said tightly, "if our goal was to overshadow the work the foundation is trying to do with some tawdry tabloid drama."

"Ah, Vanya," Nikolai said, something like a sigh in his voice, and that look in his cold blue eyes that suggested Ivan had let him down.

Again. "You don't have the guts to do this after all, do you?"

"I didn't say that."

"Your actions say it all." Nikolai shook his head. "This should not have been hard. Seduce the professor. Then finish with her as publicly as possible tonight, making certain that no one will ever take her seriously again."

"Nikolai." His own voice was harsh, but he knew it was aimed at himself. For coming up with this plan in the first place. For making it happen. For making his brother—who had been let down and lied to by everyone he'd ever known, who'd been abandoned so many times he now expected it as a matter of course, who had nothing and no one in the world except Ivan—one more promise he wanted to break. "I know the damned plan."

"You couldn't wait for her to show up in your hotel, you were so excited to enact your revenge," Nikolai said then, his voice something other than cold—which set off all kinds of alarms inside of Ivan. "You promised you would make her pay."

"You're giving me a headache," Ivan growled. "I know all of this."

"And it's already worked beautifully," Nikolai continued, unperturbed by the scowl Ivan was directing at him. "You've got your revenge. So why not drive it all the way home? The way you promised?"

Finally, something that should have been obvious from the start occurred to Ivan, and those alarms within grew louder. Deafening.

"Nikolai…" He searched his brother's face. That hard face so much like his own, those cold, broken eyes he barely recognized. "Why are you talking to me in English?"

But even as he said it, he knew.

He saw that grim, painful sort of triumph in his brother's eyes. More than that, he heard that soft sound from behind them.

He knew before he turned.

Miranda stood there, ashen. Her mouth was parted slightly, and two hectic spots of color appeared on her cheeks as she stared at him. As if he'd slapped her.

"Miranda…" he said, but she held up a hand, as if she couldn't bear it, and for a moment her lovely face crumpled in on itself. He thought it might kill him. But he knew better than to move toward her, to hold her.

"I shouldn't be surprised." Her voice was small, but it didn't shake. She looked at Nikolai briefly, then her gaze slammed into Ivan's. "I'm not surprised, as a matter of fact. It makes perfect sense that you would do exactly this. It's who you are, isn't it? You decimate your opponents. You never lose."

"Miranda," he began again. He hated that tone in her voice, that stunned sort of pain. "Please."

"And I suppose I owe it to you," she continued as if she hadn't heard him. She was standing so straight, so perfectly straight and unbearably fragile, and he had the sudden notion that she might shatter into pieces if she so much as breathed. "I've learned that, if nothing else. I was wrong about you, and I regret it." She swallowed, hard, her gaze nothing but black as she stared at him. "But I can't take it back. I can't change it. So if you have to do this thing—if you have to humiliate me in public, here…" She stopped for a moment, then sucked in a ragged-sounding breath. "If that's what you need, Ivan, I'll do it."

"This is not what I need," he said furiously, painfully. "This is not what I want."

"It's your plan," she said, so simply, so quietly, it broke his heart.

Her eyes were glazed with what he knew were tears, but she didn't cry. She only waited. For him to tell her what to do—how best to participate in her own downfall. He saw the tiniest hint of a tremor move over her, but she repressed it almost at once, and he wondered what it cost her to stand there like this—for him.

He wanted to pull her into his arms. He wanted to be the man who saved her, who protected her—not the man who hurt her. He wanted to be the man he imagined he was when she smiled at him. The kind of man who would never make her feel the way she did right now. The man he'd always thought he was, not the man she'd believed him to be all these years. He wanted to kill his own brother for putting that terrible look on her precious face. And himself for letting it happen.

"No," he said, his voice hoarse, barely a thread of sound. "It's done. There is no plan anymore."

He heard Nikolai's muttered curse in Russian, but all of his attention was on Miranda. His beautiful Miranda. She nodded once, jerkily. Then she shifted back on her heels, and he saw the way she bit her lip.

"Your brother is right," she said, her voice scratchy, as if the tears she fought back clawed at her throat. "The damage is done. You got your revenge. Congratulations."

"This is not over—"

"It is." She shook her head when he moved, almost involuntarily, and he froze. "It's finished. This was the agreement, wasn't it? This was always our last night." She started to turn, but then she looked back at him, and her dark eyes, nearly black with the pain she wasn't letting show, not completely, slapped at him. Shamed him. "Don't follow me, Ivan. Please."

And then she really did turn, and she walked away from him, head held high, as if he hadn't seen the misery he felt raging inside of him written all over her.

As if she was already well on her way to surviving this intact. Ivan couldn't say the same.

He forced a breath. Then another.

But he still wanted to rip his brother limb from limb when he turned.

Nikolai's face was shut down. Hard and blank. But Ivan knew what he hid behind it. What howled in him, tearing him to pieces from within. Tonight, he didn't care as much as he should.

"Don't forget, Vanya. I am trained to do the things others don't. Or won't." Nikolai's frosty blue eyes met his. Held. "And I always keep my promises."

Ivan knew that should have pierced him to the core. Two weeks ago, it would have swamped him with that same old guilt. But tonight he only looked at his brother and pitied him—pitied both of them. And it was nothing next to the rage he felt that Miranda was caught up in this old family mess. That it had tainted her, too.

No more. *It's not your fault*, she'd told him, and it had changed everything. Perhaps he hadn't understood how much until now. He rubbed his hands over his face.

"If you feel you have to fight me," Nikolai continued, sounding hauntingly like the little brother Ivan remembered from a world away, a lifetime ago, "I don't mind. If it helps you remember who you are."

"Kolya," he said finally, fiercely, using the family name he hadn't dared speak aloud in too many years to count.

Nikolai jerked in surprise, and for the first time, there was something other than ice in his gaze. There was a glimmer again of the brother Ivan remembered.

"You are my brother, my only family, my blood. I wish I could have protected you. I wish I could have protected myself. But you need to go and fix your life before you disappear completely. And before you destroy whatever love I have for you."

He held Nikolai's gaze, and didn't drop it when his brother's face flushed slightly, as if he'd hit him. For the first time in years, Nikolai looked uncertain. Even lost. But it was too late.

"And I don't want to see you again until you do."

CHAPTER TWELVE

ELEGANT and sophisticated, Miranda reminded herself fiercely as she jerkily removed her makeup in front of the huge bathroom mirror in Ivan's master suite, meant there would be no tears. No tears, no sobs, no crumpling into the fetal position on the bathroom floor and rocking herself for a while.

And if a tear or two leaked out while she scooped up water in her palms and washed her face, well, no one ever had to know that but her.

She was starting on her hair when Ivan appeared in the mirror behind her. She didn't hear his approach. He wasn't there, she blinked, and then he was leaning in the doorway, his black gaze hard and hurt and some kind of hungry. Her heart kicked against her ribs, hard, then seemed to drop straight down to her bare toes.

Miranda's arms dropped to her sides, letting the few pins she'd already pulled free clatter onto the granite countertop beside the sleek vertical basin of his sink. She wanted to ignore him, to bustle along with her departure, efficient and matter-of-fact, and be gone before the party was over. She'd already packed her bag. She looked almost like herself again now, in very old, very comfortable jeans that felt as close to that fetal position on the floor as she was going to get tonight, and the faded college T-shirt she slept in when she was alone. All she had to do was get her hair out of this dramatic style, slip on her shoes and leave. Simple.

But she couldn't seem to look away from Ivan's reflection.

And worse, she couldn't seem to move.

The silence seemed too large between them, too painful, and she wished she didn't love him as hopelessly and helplessly as she did. She wished she didn't notice the pain in his eyes, the way his hard mouth flattened. She wished she didn't want, even now, to turn and go to him. To comfort him.

"I meant what I said." She couldn't take the silence another second. She was too afraid of what she might do if it continued, and it had nothing to do with elegance or sophistication. "I was wrong. If you want me to take to the airwaves to say so, I will."

"I don't."

"I'm happy to do it." She curled her hands into fists, still watching him through the mirror. "If it's what you or your brother need."

Ivan pushed away from the doorjamb and prowled toward her, and she couldn't help the flush of excitement that raced through her, over her. Her body was so attuned to his, it was readying itself for his possession no matter the state of her emotions. He stopped when he was behind her, his gaze still locked on hers, and for a moment he simply stood there, so big and so dangerous behind her, and it was so much like Paris all over again that it made Miranda's chest tighten painfully. She thought she might explode, so she turned around to face him—anything to banish the memory of that dressing room—

But that was a mistake.

She was so used to touching him now. She was so used to closing small distances between them like this by simply leaning forward and into that powerful chest of his. It caused her actual, physical pain to reach behind her instead, and grip the lip of the bathroom counter.

"When did you turn passive and accommodating?" he asked quietly. "I find it terrifying."

"This is not passive, Ivan," she said, the sudden surge of temper like a shot of color through gray clouds. "This is polite. This is understanding. You said you didn't want a scene. Have you changed your mind?"

"No," he said. "But nothing else has changed, either."

She didn't understand him, until he simply reached over and slid that large hand of his over her hip, yanking her into him and taking her mouth that easily.

It was hot. It was perfect. It was Ivan.

And it hurt Miranda in ways she expected would leave scars.

She shoved him back, and he let her go, but she couldn't control the tears that welled up in her eyes then, the great storm inside of her that she'd been fighting so hard to keep hidden away.

"Is this your final little bit of revenge?" she demanded when the tears began to fall, exposing her despite everything. "You want to see me fall apart in front of you? Just let me leave, Ivan. Let me keep my promise and go."

"What if I don't want you to go?" His voice was rough, his black gaze intense.

And she realized that this, right here, was her opportunity to be strong, finally. To protect herself, at last. She wanted to believe him more than she'd ever wanted anything. She wanted it so much she thought she could *feel* that wanting on a cellular level. She wanted him, any way she could get him. She loved him. And she knew that it would be far too easy to simply allow this. To take whatever time she could with him, and bask in it and simply postpone this harsh ending for another time.

She also knew it might kill her. So she shook her head at him, and wiped at her face. And tried, for once, to be as strong as she should have been all along.

"You can have sex exactly like this with anyone in the world," she told him. "I'm sure you already have. You don't need me."

He laughed, though it was not a happy sound, and Miranda took the opportunity to duck around him and head for the dressing room and her bag. Forget her hair. She needed to get away from him while she still had some remnant of a spine.

"But you need me," he said from behind her.

She stopped walking, as surely as if he'd had her on a leash and had just yanked on it. Hard. She turned back around slowly. Incredulously.

He looked more fierce than she'd ever seen him, in that sleek tuxedo that somehow hinted at all of his ferocity while managing to make him something like elegant, too. Yet all of him devastatingly, finely honed male. That heat of his seemed to burn brighter, making her belly tighten, and her core soften, even as she stared at him as if she could not possibly have heard him correctly.

"And more than that, Miranda," he said in that way of his, a formidable punch wrapped with that Russian flavor, "you are in love with me."

The whole world collapsed, sucked into a giant black hole of her shame and horror and a sheer terror that felt a lot like some kind of exultation— but she still stood there, her bare feet against the polished floor, her face wet from her own tears, her entire life a sad, sick joke that had led straight here. To this tragic little farce.

She wanted to deny it. She wanted to scream. She wished she could simply die where she stood, saving her the trouble of attempting to survive this. She'd known for a while now that he would break her heart. She hadn't expected him to simply reach out and rip it still beating from her chest.

She should have remembered this was Ivan Korovin. He was capable of anything. That was why she loved him in the first place.

"You told me in your sleep," he said, watching her as he moved closer, a dark menace in beautiful clothes. "And you screamed it yesterday as you fell into pieces all around me."

Her heart seemed to beat with spikes attached, sending painful shock waves through her each time. She sucked in a breath, then another. And then she simply stopped fighting. What was the point? She'd already lost everything that mattered to her. The career she'd thought made her who she was, but was no more than a house of cards built on trashing this man. And now him, too, but she'd expected that. She'd signed up for it in advance. It didn't make it easier. But it was still happening.

"Yes, well." She laughed then, aware that it sounded ever so slightly hysterical against all of his white walls and moody, abstract paintings. "I've never been particularly smart, have I? Not where you're concerned."

"I don't want you to go," he said again, his voice harder this time, nearly ferocious.

And it hurt. It all just hurt.

"Because you don't know how to lose," she managed to say. "But this is how it's going to happen, whether you like it or not. Whether it breaks your undefeated record or not. This is what we agreed."

And Ivan lost his cool.

"I don't care about the agreement," he said. Though the first time he said it, he used far uglier words. "I don't care about *winning*."

But she only shook her head, unmoved despite the emotion he could see staining her face, making her stand so tautly. "Ivan—"

"You can't tell me you love me and then walk away!" he threw at her, dimly aware that he was louder than usual. Much louder than was safe. "You can't cry in my arms and tell me things you've never told another living soul and then just…go back to New York as if none of this ever happened!"

"Why not?" she demanded, her eyes too bright again, her voice rough. "It's what you want!"

"You should know by now, Miranda, that I

never get what I want," he snapped at her, totally unhinged now, completely lost to himself,
as if he'd never had any training. As if he was
nothing but this wild storm she'd made inside of
him. "I suffer. I do my duty. I win on command.
But what I want is never part of the package."

"Ivan," she began again, her voice broken, as
he surged toward her and made her back up a
few steps, as if she could see that wildness in
him. But her wide eyes, dark jade and anguished,
drank him in anyway.

"You have haunted me across years," he told
her hoarsely. "You have challenged me and pro-
voked me, and that was before I met you. I didn't
expect to like you. I didn't expect to crave you."
He wasn't shouting anymore, but it felt the same,
out of control and the closest he'd been to desperate since he was a boy. "Tell me how to let you
go, Professor. Tell me how to pretend none of this
ever happened. Tell me how to pretend that I can't
see that you hate the very idea of it yourself."

"You wanted to humiliate me in public," she
challenged. "But not in any straightforward kind
of way. You wanted to seduce me into submission first, because it would hurt more."

"You are writing a nasty, damaging book about

me," he retorted. "All insinuations and fantasies and lies. *Another* book."

"I've already told my agent it isn't happening," she snapped.

He reached over then to brush her tears from her pretty face.

"You are in love with me," he gritted out. "You don't want to do this. You don't want to go."

Her face crumpled then, and it tore at him. She raised a hand to her mouth as if that might hold her together, but still, a sob rolled out anyway and made him feel small. Mean.

"What happens if I stay, Ivan?" she asked, her voice thick. "If it hurts this much now, how much worse will it be two weeks from now? A month? I can't do it. I can't willingly subject myself—"

"You love me."

She'd said it half-asleep. She'd screamed it in the height of passion. And so it lived in Ivan like tension, and he frowned at her as if he could bend her to his will that easily. As if he could make her say it now, when it counted.

Miranda let out a sound somewhere between a sob and a sigh. Her shoulders dropped, and her head canted forward slightly, as if she'd let go of something very heavy, all at once.

"I do," she whispered. "I do love you."

And that was the last of his foundations turned into dust, just like that. Setting him free.

He swept her into his arms and held her high against him, drowning in that look on her face, as if he was the man he'd always wanted to be. As if she saw him when no one else could.

"I am a rough man," he told her fiercely. "I made myself from fists and sheer will, and that is all I know. There were no ivory towers for me. No easy escapes. I've had to fight for every single thing I have, and most of what I lost."

She reached up her hand and held his face with it, her touch somehow healing, even as another tear tracked its way down her cheek.

"I'll fight for you," she whispered.

He lost himself then in the sweet, slick heat of her mouth. In the perfection of her arms around him, her body against his, the fact that she knew him better than anyone else in the world, and she loved him anyway.

When he pulled back to breathe, they had found their way to the bed, and she wrapped herself around him as if she would never let him go.

"I want more than two weeks," he told her in a rush, things opening wide inside of him, like she was the light and all of his shadows were surrendering to her, one by one. "I want forever. Live with me. Marry me. I don't care. I want everything."

She smiled at him, that beautiful smile that changed him from the inside out, and he understood. Finally, he understood.

"I love you," he said, and the words sounded stilted. Strange. As well they should. He'd never said them before. In any language.

Or maybe it was that his life, his love, his heart—everything he was or wanted to be— hung there in those three small syllables and the woman who gazed up at him, her face scrubbed clean and her dark red hair a fierce tangle.

Her smile deepened, changed. Made new worlds, and took him with her.

"I know you do," she said softly, and then she kissed him.

Binding them together, like a tightly held fist, unbreakable and sure.

Forever.

Eighteen months later, Miranda stood in her one-bedroom apartment in New York City, wrinkling her nose as she looked around at the bare white walls. The empty floors. She stood in the center of what had been her bedroom so long ago, when she'd been a completely different person. When she'd hardly known herself. When she'd fought her nightmares nightly and alone, instead of very rarely and with Ivan. She gazed down at the simple, elegant solitaire that he'd slid onto her finger only a week ago now, when she'd finally agreed to marry him after a very long campaign.

Mostly conducted in bed, his preferred negotiation strategy.

Miranda smiled. It was time to trust. It was time to let go of fear. It was time to officially move into the sprawling penthouse on Central Park West he'd bought to be near her during the Columbia school year. It was past time.

There was no noise behind her, no sound at all, but she knew he was there. She always did. She turned slowly, and let the punch of his sheer physical presence move through her, as ever. He was big and dark, wearing a great black coat over jeans and a jacket, looking every inch the wealthy, famous man he was. Beautiful and lethal.

And hers.

"Second thoughts?" he asked, in an arrogant tone of voice that scorned the very idea.

But she knew him so well now. She knew what he hid beneath all of that bluster.

"Never," she said.

He smiled in that open, real way that still made her a little bit giddy, and nodded at the book she held in her hand.

"A memento?"

"It was stuck way back on the shelf in my closet," she said, flipping it over in her hands. It was a hardcover copy of *Caveman Worship*, the book that had started all of this. A book of lies that had led her here to the only truth that mattered. "Maybe I should leave it here. I wouldn't want you to feel you had to ritually burn it in on the terrace one night."

"Revert to my favorite judgmental professor of old, *milaya moya*, and I might burn you on the terrace instead."

"Promises, promises," she said in a singsong voice, and laughed when he walked into the room and kissed her soundly, then pulled her against him.

"How much longer will we stand here?" he

asked quietly. "We have the rest of our lives to start living, and these ghosts are not invited."

Miranda looked at the book, and felt it all move through her—the things they'd been through. The things they'd put each other through. And what they'd managed to build together out of all of it. Her latest book had been about high fashion as a cultural conversation, and no one wanted to talk about it on television shows. She'd discovered that was a relief. Instead of using entertainment gossip as a way to bludgeon Ivan, she worked with his foundation instead, creating outreach programs for juveniles in homes with domestic abuse.

And he made her forget herself whenever he touched her, and she was finally, perfectly safe. *Much better than any fairy tale*, she thought.

"Let's go," she said. She went to throw the book on the floor. "I think we're done with this."

But he stopped her, taking the book in his hand.

"I want it," he said, grinning at her. Happier and brighter in these last months than ever before. The man, he told her often, he'd always wanted to be. It made her feel like flying. Like they already were. Like together they were made of wings—and joy. "It's my favorite work of fiction."

* * * * *